THE ARMCHAIR DETECTIVE

The Armchair Detective

SERIES ONE

The Complete 'Boxed Set'

Ian Shimwell

CONTENTS

Series One

THE ARMCHAIR DETECTIVE

INTRODUCTION

A chance meeting with a mysterious elderly man...

Who is Old Tom - a sad and lonely fusspot? Or a forgotten
figure whose bewildering deductive abilities hint at something
more..?
Does he ever leave his armchair?
Why is he only seen or heard by engaging, local newspaper
reporter, Trench?
And what surprising secret are the Mayflower Court Flats
really hiding?

Come on a challenging, yet comfortable investigation.
Can you solve the mystery without leaving your armchair..?

*I am still very fond of the 'pilot' script. I feel it introduces the
main characters and sets up the format of the series nicely.
Mystery and comedy elements established. I also like that it
throws at least three avenues of investigation to further confound
(hopefully) the reader.*

CAST LIST

TRENCH

OLD TOM

SALLY-ANNE

EDITOR LAW

STONEBRIDGE

JILL MASTERSON

JENKINS

LINDA STONEBRIDGE

AGENT

TIMOTHY

ACT ONE

OPENING MYSTERY MUSIC

TRENCH: Remember, Sally-Anne, we want to speak to as many old people as possible in these flats.

SALLY-ANNE: Yes, and as I've not completely lost my marbles quite yet, please stop repeating yourself.

TRENCH: Right, you do this flat and I'll do the next one… No, I'll do this one and you do the next one.

SALLY-ANNE: Brilliant, with a mind like that, one day you will make a great journalist. I can see it now, the local newspaper hack, Trenchy Trench wins the National Associated Press award for outstanding…

TRENCH: Less of the Trenchy, I'm just Trench… and I don't think I'm going to win an award listing our mature citizen's top ten gripes, but sometimes bigeth things cometh from small stories…

SALLY-ANNE: Maybe. Why do you want to visit that flat first, anyway?

TRENCH: Call me old fashioned, Sally-Anne, but you have to start somewhere.

SALLY-ANNE: Trench, you're old fashioned – see you at the end of the row.

TRENCH: Well, here goes.

SALLY-ANNE: Wait, there's no answer and the door's naturally locked too.

(We hear SALLY-ANNE try the door.)

TRENCH: Right, well you try this one and I'll try yours then.

(They swap flats.)

(We hear TRENCH knock on the door.)

OLD VOICE: Come in, young man, the door is open.

TRENCH: (Says quietly to himself:) Funny, I thought it was locked. Twenty-two B Mayflower Court, what am I letting myself into?

(We hear an inner door creak open.)

TRENCH: I'm sorry to disturb you Mr... err? There's no need to get up from your armchair.

OLD MAN: You have not disturbed me – and I have no intention of 'getting up' as you put it. You may call me 'Old Tom' young man. Be seated.

TRENCH: Thank-you Old Tom, I'm a ...

OLD TOM: ... journalist, I know – and you are master?

TRENCH: Trench, I thought I was too old to be addressed as a master though.

OLD TOM: Compared to me, Trenchy you are not too old.

(TRENCH audibly winces at 'Trenchy'.)

TRENCH: Wait a minute, how did you know I am a journalist?

OLD TOM: There is a tell-tale notepad and pencil peeping out of your top pocket, you're manner is as condescending as I would expect from a member of your profession – and besides we were all informed by letter that members of the local Press would be here to poke their noses in.

TRENCH: Which brings me to the point of my visit, Mr Thomas...

OLD TOM: My name is 'Old' followed by 'Tom', Trench.

TRENCH: Sorry, Old Tom, then. Are you adequately looked-after? Is the warden attentive? Do Social Services visit? Do friends and relatives regularly come to see you? Are you lonely? Is the heating satisfactory? Hang-on, it's awfully cold in here – why isn't your gas fire on? Can't you afford it? Do you need more..?

OLD TOM: *(Who talks sternly with authority, instantly silencing TRENCH:)* Enough. I can afford heating – but I choose not to use it. Heating breeds bugs. I never see the warden – again by choice. I have no visitors – and I am not lonely.

TRENCH: You must be cold. Here, let me adjust your blanket.

(We hear an audible 'slap'. TRENCH quickly withdraws his hand.)

TRENCH: Ouch!

OLD TOM: Stop fussing, I am fine. You can do something for me though, if you'd be so kind, young Trench.

TRENCH: Name it Old Thomas, I mean Old Tom.

OLD TOM: My tea is on the table next to my armchair. Would you pass it to me?

TRENCH: But you can reach that, oh never mind. Here…

(We hear the slight rattle of a cup and saucer as TRENCH passes the tea to OLD TOM.)

OLD TOM: I am indebted.

TRENCH: But that tea feels stone cold.

OLD TOM: I know, just how I like it.

TRENCH: Well thank-you err… Old Tom for a most interesting conversation. I'll leave you in peace now.

OLD TOM: Wait. Have you not, at least, wondered why you've been given such an 'exciting' assignment?

TRENCH: It's simply routine. Elderly people complaining about their standard of care, sells local papers, would you believe?

OLD TOM: Yes, but why here? Your editor plays golf with Councillor Stonebridge, does he not?

TRENCH: How on earth do you know that?

OLD TOM: Why does Stonebridge want to stir up trouble in these humble block of flats?

TRENCH: I didn't know he did, but I suppose it's a possibility.

OLD TOM: There are a lot of questions to ask in this matter. You are a journalist, Trench, so start asking…

TRENCH: I'll… I'll look into it.

OLD TOM: And when you have, my boy – you may report back to me.

(There is a slight, amused chuckle at the back of

TRENCH's throat.)

TRENCH: Of course.

                (*There is a short play of whimsical music indicating a slight passage of time*.)

TRENCH: Don't you just love it, Sally-Anne, being in the very heart of journalistic dynamism?

SALLY-ANNE: What, a pokey office with two desks shoehorned inside, situated in the back streets of Stokeham? Doesn't exactly fill me of inspiration.

TRENCH: That's what the motto of the Stokeham Herald should be: 'Be inspired'.

SALLY-ANNE: (*Who gives a snort of derision*:) Yeah right, anyway I think a car manufacturer or a computer company has beaten you to that one. You know, copyright and all that.

TRENCH: Just a thought.

SALLY-ANNE: Well I'm too tired to think – I must have visited over sixty flats on Mayflower Court. How many did you visit, Trenchy?

TRENCH: Just the one.

SALLY-ANNE: Most complain they haven't enough money for heating; they either need a new bed or chamber pot; the warden appears to be the invisible man; the walls are literally crumbling; the flats are damp and draughty and, by the way, it's hard to get a decent chiropodist these days... Excuse me, did I hear you right – you only visited one while I worked through over sixty of the over-sixties?

TRENCH: We... err... we got talking.

SALLY-ANNE: I'll say you did. What were you discussing, the merits of 'War and Peace'?

TRENCH: His name is 'Old Tom' and he suggested that Councillor Stonebridge somehow persuaded our illustrious Editor, John Law to put us on this little assignment.

SALLY-ANNE: That's ridiculous. Why would Stonebridge even do that? Could he influence our editor, anyway? Are you sure your new friend still has all his marbles?

TRENCH: He knew that Editor Law and Stonebridge were acquainted. He even knew that they play golf together.

SALLY-ANNE: Oh come on, that's easy. Don't you ever read our own newspaper? Just look at page fifteen of last week's edition.

(We hear the rustle of the paper, as TRENCH turns to the page.)

TRENCH: Ah, I see it. Councillor and local businessman, Sam Stonebridge beats Herald Editor John Law in club, charity golf tournament…

SALLY-ANNE: I think, perhaps Trench, you were taken in by his, say, mysterious manner?

TRENCH: Yes, I suppose it's not exactly deduction on the Sherlock Holmes scale, is it?

SALLY-ANNE: Did he ask you to go back and report on progress, by any chance?

TRENCH: (*Says hesitantly:*) Yes.

SALLY-ANNE: I knew it. Old Tommy, I'm afraid, is just a sad, lonely old man simply looking for an excuse for some company.

TRENCH: You're probably right.

SALLY-ANNE: So, are you going to chase wild geese, and follow up this Stonebridge thing?

TRENCH: (*Who laughs slightly.*) Not a chance.

(A short passage of music indicates a change of scene and time.)

TRENCH: Excuse me, would it be possible to see Mr Stonebridge, Miss..?

JILL MASTERSON: Ms Jill Masterson actually – and no it would not be possible. Mr Stonebridge is a very busy man who only sees people strictly by appointment.

TRENCH: Well, you see I'm… err Trench and am on an errand from my editor John Law who's a good friend of your Mr Stonebridge…

JILL MASTERSON: Fascinating…

TRENCH: They recently played a charity game of golf.

JILL MASTERSON: Mr Trench, are you trying to bore me to death?

TRENCH: And to cut a long story short, Ms Masterson - old Stonebridge lost one of his golf balls which has since been recovered…

JILL MASTERSON: (*Who rudely stifles a yawn.*) Balls.

TRENCH: … and I'd like to return it. You know how fussy golfers can be about this sort of thing?

JILL MASTERSON: No, I don't. Give me your ball and I will return it at my earliest convenience.

TRENCH: My instructions were to return said ball personally.

(*At that moment, we hear the office door open.*)

STONEBRIDGE: Ah Jill, hold all calls. I'm going on an early lunch. I'm aware you are leaving soon, yourself.

JILL MASTERSON: At once, Sam… sir.

TRENCH: I was just saying to Jill here, is it possible, Mr Stonebridge, to have a quick chat about the Mayflower Court flats? I'm Trench from the Stokeham Herald.

JILL MASTERSON: *(Says just loudly enough for TRENCH to hear:)* As I said, balls.

STONEBRIDGE: Damned if I know what you're talking about, err Trench – but you may talk while I walk, if you wish. I'm a busy man.

TRENCH: As I've gathered. Thank-you sir.

(There are several opening and closing of doors as TRENCH follows STONEBRIDGE out. We can hear the hustle and bustle of the small town, the pedestrians and traffic in the background.)

STONEBRIDGE: You were lucky to find anyone in, I'm away at a council meeting this afternoon, in fact even Jill – my secretary you understand, has the rest of the day off.

TRENCH: Really, Mr Stonebridge?

STONEBRIDGE: Trench, isn't it? Damn queer name if you ask me. Ah yes, Jill – it's the anniversary of her father's death. Thirty years I believe, tragic business.

TRENCH: Death usually is.

(We hear the beep beep of a Pelican crossing.)

STONEBRIDGE: What did you say?

TRENCH: Oh, nothing.

STONEBRIDGE: Excuse me, Mr Trench but you did say you wanted to talk about the Mayflower flats.

TRENCH: I did – and still do.

STONEBRIDGE: I'd be intrigued to know my connection in all this.

TRENCH: Can I ask what your business is – and your role as a Councillor?

STONEBRIDGE: It's no secret, I suppose. I am a property developer – and oversee the planning applications at the Town Hall.

(TRENCH coughs in disbelief.)

TRENCH: And you don't see there is a conflict of interests in that?

STONEBRIDGE: *(Says sternly:)* I make sure there isn't. A polite warning young man – do not attempt to cross me Trench, it would not be worth your while.

TRENCH: Relax sir, I was just checking.

STONEBRIDGE: *(Says with mounting frustration:)* And the flats?

TRENCH: Oh, yes. My colleague and I, that is we were asked – I mean checked on the concerns of the in-mates, I mean inhabitants of Mayflower Court.

STONEBRIDGE: And?

TRENCH: Do you know anybody in your professional or public life that is looking for an excuse to get rid of those flats?

STONEBRIDGE: Life moves on, Trench. None of us can stand still. Progress can often mean the destruction of say 'derelict' flats...

TRENCH: The Mayflower land would be a prime site for development being close to the town centre... Are you sure you don't know anybody, Mr Stonebridge?

STONEBRIDGE: No, I don't – and now here's my beautiful wife, Linda. So, if you don't mind..?

TRENCH: (*Says quietly*:) She is beautiful – and much younger than him.

LINDA STONEBRIDGE: I've not had the pleasure.

(*TRENCH clears his throat, displaying his amused embarrassment.*)

TRENCH: Neither have I – I'm Trench and am about to take my leave. If you'll forgive me.

LINDA STONEBRIDGE: (*Says slightly in awe*:) Who was that?

STONEBRIDGE: A troublemaker.

(*More music and a change of scene and time.*)

TRENCH: So, Mr Old Tom – that's all I can tell you about my meeting with our friend, Sam Stonebridge.

OLD TOM: Interesting, very interesting... You did report back to me though, Trench – thank-you.

TRENCH: What can I say; I'm a man of my word.

OLD TOM: So I see. Would you be so kind to pass me a piece of cake?

(*We hear a slight clatter of the plate as TRENCH passes the cake.*)

TRENCH: Do you actually ever get up from that armchair of yours?

OLD TOM: (*Who chuckles softly.*) Oh yes, I do, my boy – but only very, very rarely.

(*OLD TOM munches on his cake.*)

TRENCH: Why did you think my chat with Stonebridge was 'interesting'? Getting back to the matter in hand.

OLD TOM: You don't waste much time with chitchat, do you Trenchy?

TRENCH: I try not to.

OLD TOM: There finished. That cake was completely crusty and stale – and the cream had gone off – just how I like it.

TRENCH: (*Says resignedly*:) Do you want me to pass your tea?

OLD TOM: No, not yet – at the moment it'll be far too warm.

TRENCH: I see – no I don't, but as you were saying, Tom about 'interesting'..? (*Then says quietly to himself*:) What in the name of 'Scoop of the Year' made me return to this luxury penthouse?

OLD TOM: More of the 'Old' please.

TRENCH: (*Who sighs*.) I'm sorry – Old Tom that is.

OLD TOM: First, young Trench, I want to hear your conclusions about this lark so far.

TRENCH: Lark? (*TRENCH sniggers slightly*.) I suppose it is. I don't think there is any great mystery here. It is obvious to me that Stonebridge would like this Mayflower site to become 'available'. Evidence suggests that he has already abused his position as Councillor to put pressure on certain people and eventually acquire the land and then make a huge profit.

OLD TOM: Very good, my boy, carry on.

TRENCH: You and all the other residents will be forced to move, whether you want to or not.

OLD TOM: I like it here.

TRENCH: And I think Stonebridge persuaded his friend – my editor to do an exposé: how terrible the flats are etcetera, to instigate the whole murky process.

OLD TOM: So, Mr Stonebridge is public enemy number one then?

TRENCH: I think so, Old Tom – don't you?

OLD TOM: Oh yes, I agree Stonebridge is after these flats or rather the land, but I think there is more to it than that.

TRENCH: You do?

OLD TOM: If you wanted to purchase something, dodgy shall we say, on the quiet – would you make such a song and dance about it? Why publicise the faults of Mayflower Court? You could stir up a hornet's nest with do-gooders and so on. Stonebridge, in his position, could quite easily acquire this land hush, hush and at the drop of a hat with his connections.

TRENCH: So why, indirectly, encourage us to poke our noses in? Maybe he didn't, maybe it's all a coincidence.

OLD TOM: I don't do coincidences.

TRENCH: But what should I do about it now?

OLD TOM: Grasp hold of the bag of marbles and shake them up a bit. See what happens.

TRENCH: Stir things up? All right, I will.

OLD TOM: But be careful, Trench, sometimes a marble falls out of the bag – and shatters on the floor.

TRENCH: I'll have to make sure I'm not that particular marble, then.

OLD TOM: I think I'll have that tea now; it should be nice and cold. Pass it, will you?

(A longer piece of mystery music indicates the end of Act One.)

ACT TWO

SALLY-ANNE: You've been to see Sam Stonebridge, haven't you, Trench?

TRENCH: Calm down, Sally-Anne - it was only for a little chat.

SALLY-ANNE: I don't think our editor will see it that way. I'd keep my head down, if I was you - he'll be on the warpath.

TRENCH: In that case, you'll see me hide behind my desk every time he walks past then.

SALLY-ANNE: And you promised not to see Stonebridge, anyway.

TRENCH: I didn't, I just said I wouldn't follow this story up - that's all.

SALLY-ANNE: Well, you have followed it up.

TRENCH: You know what it's like when you have a

hunch, don't you? No, sorry you don't - you have to rely on women's intuition.

SALLY-ANNE:　　　　　Be careful, Trenchy.

(SALLY-ANNE sighs.)

SALLY-ANNE:　　　　　Listen, I advise you to drop it. Winding Stonebridge up will only get you sacked.

TRENCH:　　　　　I can't.

SALLY-ANNE:　　　　　What are you, an old folk's home revolutionary or something?

TRENCH:　　　　　No.

SALLY-ANNE:　　　　　Got it, you've been to see Old Tommy again, haven't you? He's put you up to this.

TRENCH:　　　　　I might have, it's not a crime.

SALLY-ANNE:　　　　　I feel sorry for you, Trench. You're hanging your own career out to dry, to fuel an old man's fantasies.

TRENCH:　　　　　His name is Old Tom, actually.

SALLY-ANNE:　　　　　Old Tom? I've never heard anything so ridiculous.

TRENCH:　　　　　What have you got against him?

(From several offices away, there is an almighty bellow.)

EDITOR LAW:　　　　　Trench, my office - now!

SALLY-ANNE:　　　　　I think our esteemed boss is requesting the pleasure of your company.

TRENCH:　　　　　Really, I hadn't noticed - but I think I'll go and check, just in case.

SALLY-ANNE: You do that. *(SALLY-ANNE sighs in an amused fashion.)*

(TRENCH joins EDITOR LAW in the office.)

EDITOR LAW: Close the door, Trench.

(We hear TRENCH shut the door.)

EDITOR LAW: Sit.

TRENCH: Thank-you, Editor Law.

EDITOR LAW: If I remember rightly, I simply requested that you asked some old dears some questions, not upset my golfing partner. Why have you upset my golfing partner?

TRENCH: I - I didn't mean to. The story just kind of lead to Mr. Stonebridge.

EDITOR LAW: So, the story is to blame - not you. *(Then says impatiently:)* Why did the story lead to Sam, err Stonebridge?

TRENCH: It seems there is a connection between pressure for the Mayflower to go and your friend's acquisition of the land.

EDITOR LAW: Oh, grow up, Trench, the council simply doesn't have the resources to restore those flats, so Stonebridge - or someone like him will always profit from change.

TRENCH: You're probably right.

EDITOR LAW: Is it because you've befriended an old gentleman who lives in the flats?

TRENCH: How did you..?

EDITOR LAW: Sally-Anne let it slip.

TRENCH: I must thank her later.

EDITOR LAW: Need I say anymore, Trench?

TRENCH: No, Editor Law, you don't - but can I ask you one thing: Did Stonebridge suggest this paper quiz the Mayflower residents about their complaints?

EDITOR LAW: *(Who takes a deep breath to calm himself.)*
Yes, yes he did.

TRENCH: I knew it - but there still could be more to it...

EDITOR LAW: Oh, pursue this madness if you must - just keep Sam Stonebridge out of it - and don't bother him again. Understand?

TRENCH: You're the boss.

(A change of music indicates a change of scene and time.)

(There is a knock and the front door opens.)

TRENCH: Sorry, to bother you, Mrs Stonebridge.

LINDA STONEBRIDGE: Oh Linda, please.

TRENCH: I was wondering if your husband was at home at the moment?

LINDA STONEBRIDGE: Oh you're Trench, that reporter fellow, aren't you? Do come in.

(We hear the shuffling of footsteps as TRENCH enters - and the door closing.)

TRENCH: Yes, we briefly met the other day.

LINDA STONEBRIDGE: Do sit down on my lovely sofa - there. Well, I'm sorry but Sam is away on business - is there anything I can do for you?

TRENCH: I'm trying not to think… Err, it's late afternoon, yet you're still wearing your nightdress.

LINDA STONEBRIDGE: What's the point in changing if you have nowhere to go - and your husband is 'working late'?

TRENCH: Where is he, actually?

LINDA STONEBRIDGE: Strangely, he said some senior civil servant from the Foreign Office had summoned him for a meeting, but by now, he's probably being intimate with that tart of a secretary of his.

TRENCH: Jill Masterson.

LINDA STONEBRIDGE: Maybe she sees him as some sort of replacement father-figure seeing as she's never really had one.

TRENCH: You are pretty young too actually and pretty.

LINDA STONEBRIDGE: How sweet - but my main attraction for Sam is his money. Now, you on the other hand…

TRENCH: You mean..?

LINDA STONEBRIDGE: Yes, I am already in a state of undress - let's make things more even.

TRENCH: Hadn't we better go…

LINDA STONEBRIDGE: …upstairs? I'm already ahead of you.

(We hear them scramble upstairs.)

TRENCH: Oh, Linda.

(We hear them kissing.)

LINDA STONEBRIDGE: Oh, Trench.

(We hear the front door opening.)

TRENCH: Oh, God.

STONEBRIDGE: *(Who SHOUTS:)* Linda, Linda where are you? Come on, I won't be in long.

TRENCH: I don't think your wardrobe is big enough to hide in. *(Then says, irritably:)* You said he was out.

LINDA STONEBRIDGE: Well now he's back in. Quick, I'll see to him in the living room, while you slip out through the kitchen.

STONEBRIDGE: *(Who now almost roars:)* Linda!

LINDA STONEBRIDGE: Stop shouting honey, I'm coming.

(More music, this time with a lighter note. Again, the scene and time move on.)

SALLY-ANNE: Where the hell have you been all afternoon?

TRENCH: Good afternoon Trench, how are you?

SALLY-ANNE: Well?

TRENCH: You don't want to know.

SALLY-ANNE: I do want to know - and you are going to tell me. You've not been to see Stonebridge again, have you?

TRENCH: Not exactly - he was out as I suspected he would be, but his wife was in.

SALLY-ANNE: So, you had a cosy chat then?

TRENCH: You could say that...

SALLY-ANNE: Do you like the smudged lipstick look?

TRENCH: Oh no.

(We hear TRENCH furiously trying to rub the lipstick off.)

SALLY-ANNE: Pathetic, Trenchy.

TRENCH: What's wrong Sally? Jealous, are we?

SALLY-ANNE: You are supposed to be on a story. Look around at our messy desks, the Stokeham Herald won't write itself.

TRENCH: I did actually discover one useful thing, Sally of the Anne.

SALLY-ANNE: Such as..?

TRENCH: Stonebridge appears to be having an affair with his secretary.

SALLY-ANNE: That might explain his wife's strange behaviour towards you - what's sauce for the goose is sauce for the gander - that sort of thing.

TRENCH: Thanks, Sall.

SALLY-ANNE: But I don't see how it helps the Mayflower flats situation - it may give the secretary more influence though...

TRENCH: And a motive for his wife to cause trouble...

SALLY-ANNE: I'm becoming confused about these flats - you said Stonebridge wants them demolished for his eventual profit.

TRENCH: Yes, but I think there might be someone else subtlety at work behind-the-scenes trying to keep Mayflower Court exactly where it is, for reason or reasons unknown. And, I may have a lead on that...

SALLY-ANNE:	Well, are you going to tell me, Trench or are you going to continue looking like a smug bar-steward?

TRENCH:	Linda, err Stonebridge's wife also told me that her 'beloved' Sam had been summoned to a meeting at the Foreign Office, no less.

SALLY-ANNE:	You think there could be a connection? A conspiracy, an expose exclusive on the government? Our careers could shoot into orbit after this; I would be a leading writer for The Observer while you might be a tabloid hack for The Sun.

TRENCH:	Your faith in me is touching.

SALLY-ANNE:	I have a contact at the Town Hall who might be able to help us. Come on, he usually works late, we might be able to catch him.

TRENCH:	I thought you said this was all a wild goose chase?

SALLY-ANNE:	That was then, this is now.

TRENCH:	Oh, thank-you, by the way Sally-Anne for informing our editor about my chats with Old Tommy, err Old Tom.

SALLY-ANNE:	What are friends for?

(Faster paced music illustrates another change of scene and time.)

(We hear TRENCH and SALLY-ANNE walking down the corridors of the Town Hall.)

TRENCH:	I thought we'd have trouble getting in the Town Hall at this time.

SALLY-ANNE:	I know, thank goodness for council-friendly Press Passes.

TRENCH: Wait, listen - I can hear something.

(They stop - a couple's heavy breathing can be heard.)

SALLY-ANNE: *(Says quietly:)* I think it's coming from the next office. The door's ajar.

TRENCH: *(Also says quietly:)* I'll just have a peep. *(And then says slightly too loudly:)* Stonebridge! Making out on the photocopier!

SALLY-ANNE: Shhh. Here let's have a look. He's with his secretary, I presume.

TRENCH: Jill Masterson. All right, I exaggerated about the photocopier.

SALLY-ANNE: Well, now we know they are definitely seeing each other! But how do we get past the door without being spotted?

TRENCH: And if Stonebridge sees us, we will be out of here and out of a job - that is Editor Law's editor's law.

SALLY-ANNE: Oh come on, let's just walk past. I'm sure their minds are on other things at present.

(We hear their quickened steps as they carefully dash past the door.)

SALLY-ANNE: Right, now Timothy's office which should be just... here.

TRENCH: Oh, Timothy is it?

SALLY-ANNE: Please grow up Trench.

(There is a knock and the door opens.)

TIMOTHY: Sally - hi, and Trench, I assume.

SALLY-ANNE: Hi Timothy. We're here for some info on

Mayflower Court.

TIMOTHY: Like what?

TRENCH: Anything Tim, it might be something on the
site of Mayflower Court, something before even the flats were built,
perhaps.

SALLY-ANNE: And if that something involves the Foreign
Office - then bingo!

TIMOTHY: Let's have a look on the old computer then.

(We hear TIMOTHY tapping away on his computer.)

TIMOTHY: I'll cross-reference the age of the Mayflower
flats - thirty years incidentally - with any significant local activity.
Interesting… a wholesale jeweler was robbed in the same year. Let's
go back further… There was an incident, on the actual Mayflower site,
during the latter stages of the Second World War.

TRENCH: What sort of 'incident'?

TIMOTHY: I can't tell you - the information is security
protected. Could be sensitive…

SALLY-ANNE: But, with the Freedom of Information Act -
that's ridiculous.

TIMOTHY: All I'm getting is: 'Access denied' reason:
'National Security'.

SALLY-ANNE: How odd.

TRENCH: And how could a security issue from over sixty
years ago, somehow pose a threat today..?

(More mystery music ends this scene, and time moves on again.)

(We hear TRENCH walking along one of the balcony corridors of

Mayflower Court.)

TRENCH: I certainly have a lot to tell Old Tommy.

JENKINS: Excuse me sir, may I ask your business?

TRENCH: I'm Trench, a reporter with the Stokeham Herald.

JENKINS: Really?

TRENCH: I'm here to see Old Tom.

JENKINS: Old Tom? Never heard of him.

TRENCH: Here, look - here's my Press Pass, if you don't believe me.

JENKINS: Yes, I see. I'm sorry - old habits die hard. I'm an ex-police officer - Sergeant actually. Jenkins at your service.

TRENCH: Retired?

JENKINS: No, I just decided to leave - pressure and all that. It was an awful long time ago - at least three decades have been and gone...

TRENCH: Well, if you'll excuse me.

JENKINS: I remember now, you were here the other day with a young lady - err Sally-Anne, that was her name.

TRENCH: I was - but I'm afraid, Jenkins, I am going to have to dash...

JENKINS: She was asking questions about the state of this place. Well, I'll tell you what I told her...

TRENCH: *(Who says resignedly:)* Very well then, if you must.

JENKINS: The communal areas are filthy; the rooms are damp and cold; the wallpaper is either torn or coming off; the lift doesn't work and the whole place smells of something.

TRENCH: (Who sniffs.) Can't say I've noticed. So, apart from that, the flats are all right..?

JENKINS: If you ask me, Trench - these whole flats should be bulldozed down immediately. If something's rotten - get rid, that's what I say - the sooner the better.

TRENCH: But this... Mayflower Court is your home.

JENKINS: That's easy for you to say, you don't have to live here.

TRENCH: What about the people who do want to stay here?

JENKINS: Soft in the head, must be. I want one of those new, apartment-style flats nearby - once I've said good riddance to the dead Mayflower.

TRENCH: I'll pass on your comments, goodbye.

(TRENCH hurries away, climbs a set of stairs and knocks on a familiar door.)

OLD TOM: Come in, young man, the door is open.

(A piece of more gentle music signifies the passage of a relatively short period of time.)

OLD TOM: So, the plot thickens...

TRENCH: ... and becomes murkier.

OLD TOM: (Who chuckles.) I assume Mrs Stonebridge is rather good-looking then...

TRENCH: Now, you couldn't possibly know about that...

OLD TOM: There is still a sliver of lipstick right on the
corner of your mouth.

TRENCH: Oh. *(He wipes it off with his finger.)* There's
certainly nothing wrong with your eyesight.

OLD TOM: I presumed it wasn't your colleague, Sally-
Anne.

TRENCH: No, she isn't the kissing type. At least as far as
I'm concerned.

OLD TOM: Pass me a rich tea biscuit, will you?

TRENCH: Here, you're not going to dunk it? You are
going to dunk it.

OLD TOM: The question is: Who wants Mayflower Court
to remain - and why?

TRENCH: Can I suggest you pull your biscuit out? It'll go
all soggy and fall apart.

OLD TOM;   That's just how I like it.

TRENCH: I should have guessed.

OLD TOM: Is Stonebridge who, as you said Trench, like
Jenkins wants the Mayflower pulled out like a weed, somehow being
maneuvered into saving these flats - my home?

TRENCH: I think so, but who by?

OLD TOM: By whom, dear boy, by whom. Possibly his
wife, just to annoy him; his mistress stroke secretary might have her
own agenda or Stonebridge himself may be playing some sort of
double-game.

TRENCH: Or a government conspiracy stretching back to World War Two may have, financially, persuaded Stonebridge to slyly keep the flats standing.

OLD TOM: Another intriguing possibility, Trench. Do you still have your bag of marbles?

TRENCH: I haven't lost them, if that's what you mean, old timer.

OLD TOM: Good, because you will need all of them. We are entering the final phase of our investigation; more secrets will be uncovered...

TRENCH: So, what next?

OLD TOM: Pass me another biscuit, will you?

(A longer piece of mystery music indicates the end of Act Two.)

ACT THREE

(We hear TRENCH and SALLY-ANNE shuffling papers around and typing on keyboards at their desks.)

TRENCH: It's all a horrible mess. It seems there are so many people with a motive for either the Mayflower flats to be saved or erased. Maybe they are all involved...

SALLY-ANNE: ... or none of them.

TRENCH: Exactly.

SALLY-ANNE: I think the most likely 'suspect' is the Foreign Office. Governments can sink awfully low to preserve their petty secrets.

TRENCH: Yes, even a secret from so long ago. So, I'll target the Foreign Office next - any ideas on how to actually do that?

SALLY-ANNE: My contact, Timothy can probably arrange an appointment to see a civil servant close to the Foreign Secretary.

TRENCH: Right, we'll go and see him right away then.

SALLY-ANNE: Not we and not me - I've these features to
type up. Editor Law will kill me if I don't finish them. In fact you are
supposed to be doing these too.

TRENCH: So, I'd better disappear before he turns up.
Bye, my sweet Sally Anne.

SALLY-ANNE: See you, Trench-head.

*(The office door shuts sharply and a brief bit of up-tempo music passes
some more time.)*

*(TRENCH is walking along a busy street and we hear all the associated
sounds with that.)*

TRENCH: Typical, just when I want to cross the road, a
car slows down and stops right in front of me.

*(We hear the four car doors open almost at the same time and heavy
footsteps.)*

TRENCH: What do you guys want? Hey, leave me alone.

*(A protesting TRENCH is bundled into the car. The doors are slammed
shut and the car drives off at speed.)*

TRENCH: I assume you've not kidnapped me to ask
directions, so what's this all about?

AGENT: We simply want to have a little chat. You have
been asking some very awkward questions.

TRENCH: If it's not too rude an enquiry, who are you?

AGENT: I could tell you my name, but then I would
have to kill you.

TRENCH: (Who laughs nervously.) I don't think names
are important, anyway - I mean who cares? I don't know your name
and you don't know mine - I call that fair.

AGENT: You are Trench, a reporter for the Stokeham
Herald. You enjoy the old Sherlock Holmes films… I could go on. We
know all about you.

TRENCH: Correction then, you do know my name… and
my guilty secret. Can you tell me where you guys are from? Are you
something to do with the Foreign Office?

(The AGENT exhales a slightly ironic breath.)

AGENT: Yes, you could say we are something to do
with the Foreign Office…

TRENCH: Well, I'm glad that's cleared up then. This has
been awfully nice, but I really must be going. Goodbye.

(TRENCH tries to open the door as the car stops at the traffic lights, but
finds it to be locked.)

TRENCH: On second thoughts, why not stay for a bit
longer and have that cosy chat you promised me? Where are we
going?

AGENT: To a very, very quiet place…

(The car drives for a bit longer and then, finally stops.)

TRENCH: So, we've arrived - a disused and derelict
industrial estate. Can I start panicking now? Are you going to kill me?

AGENT: If we had wanted you dead, you already
would be. We simply want a quiet chat, free from interruption.

TRENCH: So, what are we going to talk about? The FA
Cup shock last night?

AGENT: Your enquiries concerning Mayflower Court.

TRENCH: How do you even know about that?

AGENT: We have our means and methods.

TRENCH: Oh, very helpful.

AGENT: We are actually here to give you some information.

TRENCH: Really? Fire away then - if you'll excuse the expression.

AGENT: It involves the incident at, what was to be, the Mayflower Court site - in the very last days of the Second World War. Accepted wisdom, claimed Hitler's experimental V3 rockets never existed, but one such rocket actually reached this country - and landed...

TRENCH: ... on the Mayflower site!

AGENT: Fortunately, the rocket did not detonate. Half of southern England would have been devastated if it had. A secret government war recovery team removed and disarmed the bomb.

TRENCH: Interesting... but all you're really telling me is that now you have no interest in the Mayflower flats. You don't really care if they stand or fall.

AGENT: Correct.

TRENCH: But how can I believe you? Maybe you're telling me this just to shut me up. A cover story for a cover-up.

AGENT: We anticipated your doubting nature, so here are several top-secret pictures and reports confirming what I have stated. You will notice that certain documents are countersigned by Churchill himself.

(TRENCH examines the pictures and reports.)

TRENCH: It appears that you are telling the truth.

AGENT: You have a pleasant head, Trench - hang on to it. Now, you can go.

TRENCH: Right, bye bye then.

AGENT: Just one more thing, Trench, before you leave.

TRENCH: Yes?

AGENT: Can we have our secret papers back? They are still kind of rather important to us.

TRENCH: Oh yes, of course.

(TRENCH hands the papers back. The door opens and TRENCH climbs out of the car - the door closes.)

TRENCH: Wait a minute, you're not leaving me here. I'm miles away from anywhere.

(His only answer is the car driving away.)

TRENCH: Oh, thanks a bunch.

(More music illustrates TRENCH's long trek back.)

SALLY-ANNE: You look exhausted, Trench. Where've you been?

TRENCH: *(Who breathes heavily.)* You really, really, do not want to know this time.

SALLY-ANNE: Quick, Editor Law's coming. Sit behind your desk and pretend you've been working all morning.

TRENCH: Oh, very well.

(TRENCH struggles behind his desk and makes the pretense of being in the middle of a lot of work by shuffling his papers around loudly.)

EDITOR LAW: Ah, Trench - good to see you doing some work, for a change.

TRENCH: Good morning, sir.

EDITOR LAW: Have you finished those features yet, Sally-Anne?

SALLY-ANNE: Yes, here they are. I couldn't have finished them without Trench's invaluable help though.

EDITOR LAW: Right, thanks err keep up the good work. *(But then adds sternly:)* Do keep away from old Stonebridge though.

TRENCH: The thought never entered my head...

(We hear EDITOR LAW leave the office.)

TRENCH: Thanks, Sally-Anne.

SALLY-ANNE: So, what really happened to you?

TRENCH: I really cannot tell you - official secrets and all that twaddle. But I can tell you that the government conspiracy theory dating back to the Second World War is completely irrelevant to our Mayflower flats investigation.

SALLY-ANNE: How can you know for sure?

TRENCH: I've seen the evidence; now trust me that line of inquiry is now over.

SALLY-ANNE: Which, I suppose, leaves us with our usual suspects.

TRENCH: Well, seeing as I've worked so hard on those features all morning...

SALLY-ANNE: A-hem.

TRENCH: I think I'll have another chat with Old Tom. I'm sure we are close to cracking this case, just need to think...

SALLY-ANNE: Seeing good Old Tom? Can I come too?

TRENCH: *(Says firmly :)* No.

SALLY-ANNE: Oh.

TRENCH: I mean, it's just a man thing. You understand, don't you?

SALLY-ANNE: Male-bonding or something more... For all I know, this Old Tom may not even exist. I've never seen him. He could be your imaginary friend. A figment of your over-active imagination.

(There is a slight shuffle of movement.)

SALLY-ANNE: Ouch! What did you pinch me for?

TRENCH: I was just checking that you were really real.

SALLY-ANNE: Beast!

(We hear SALLY-ANNE playfully slap TRENCH.)

(More music moves the scene and time along.)

OLD TOM: Hmm, this bread and jam is lovely.

TRENCH: Don't tell me Old Tom: the bread is stale - and the jam is well past its sell-by-date.

OLD TOM: You are learning, my boy. Would you put my plate back on my table?

TRENCH: Here.

(We hear TRENCH place the plate back on the table.)

OLD TOM: Now, back to business. I have pieced together
everything you have told me - and nearly, very nearly have the
solution to the Mayflower mystery. I think I   know who - but the
why, I can only guess at.

TRENCH: You do know who? Who?

OLD TOM: Oh come on, Trench. You have all the jigsaw
pieces - you just need to place them in the right order. Think, think
about all the people in this case...

TRENCH: Stonebridge; Editor Law I suppose; Jill
Masterson ... and Linda Stonebridge of course.

OLD TOM: Do not forget young Timothy and ex-Sergeant
Jenkins.

TRENCH: Why them in particular?

OLD TOM: Think, think about the information they've
told you. Information that you have already passed on to me...

TRENCH: Err...

OLD TOM: Come on. Think, Trench, think. How long...
since the Mayflower was 'planted'?

TRENCH: Yes! That's it - of course. The answer to the
Mayflower has been staring me in the face. The only thing that eludes
me, is the final answer...

OLD TOM: Then go - go and get it.

*(More music illustrates the quickening of pace and the building of
suspense.)*

TRENCH: Leave your coffee, Sally-Anne we're leaving.

SALLY-ANNE: What, now?

TRENCH: Now.

(The music plays even faster. Scene and time move on.)

TRENCH: *(Says emphasizing the 'Ms':)* Ms Masterson.

JILL MASTERSON: Ace reporter, Trench and..?

SALLY-ANNE: ...Sally-Anne.

JILL MASTERSON: *(Says with evident sarcasm:)* Stonebridge will be pleased to see you...

(The door opens.)

STONEBRIDGE: Thanks, Jill - no, he is far from pleased. How long do you plan to harass me over those damned flats? True, I admit it would make great business sense for them to come down... So, what is the problem?

TRENCH: The problem is... there are other considerations - am I right?

STONEBRIDGE: What are you talking about?

TRENCH: I wasn't talking to you, Mr Stonebridge, on that occasion. I was talking to you... Jill Masterson.

JILL MASTERSON: *(Who laughs.)* Have you completely gone out of your mind, Mr Trench? I think it's time for you to leave.

TRENCH: Time? Yes, time - it is very important.

JILL MASTERSON: Will you throw him out, Sam - or shall I?

STONEBRIDGE: May as well let him have his say now - and then we'll throw him out. And have words with his editor...

TRENCH: Thank-you Mr Stonebridge. Where was I? Ah yes, time. It is thirty years since the Mayflower flats were built; thirty years since Sergeant Jenkins left the Police Force - and thirty years since your father died, Jill. Also, by coincidence, thirty years have passed since there was a diamond heist in this area. Jill, is there a connection? Tell us the connection? Please...

(There is a moment of expectant silence.)

JILL MASTERSON: *(Who sighs.)* All right, I'll tell you then. Yes, yes there is a connection. My father was a career criminal - and he became an unofficial partner of, bent copper, Sergeant Jenkins. Together, they masterminded a relatively big job - and robbed a stash of diamonds from an export jeweler. The 'loot' was buried under what is now Mayflower Court. While my father was being 'questioned' by Jenkins - he died in police custody. Jenkins, the greedy...

TRENCH: Which leaves Jenkins to have the diamonds all to himself.

JILL MASTERSON: Only that, he couldn't. When Jenkins went to claim the diamonds, the foundations of Mayflower Court had already been laid.

TRENCH: That explains an awful lot...

JILL MASTERSON: I cannot even remember seeing my father... and although I can never prove that Jenkins was responsible for his death - I can do the next best thing: Ensure the Mayflower flats remain standing, so ex-Sergeant Jenkins can never get his dirty hands on the jewels. It pleases me to know that he knows where the diamonds are - but cannot touch them.

STONEBRIDGE: So, was that the only reason for our affair, Jill? To encourage me to influence their editor to stir up trouble over them damned flats?

JILL MASTERSON: It was at first - but funnily enough, Sam... you were actually very good. I quite enjoyed our many sessions...

SALLY-ANNE: Very good, eh? I don't suppose you are free any spare night, Mr Stonebridge? We could go for a meal or something and then, and then...

TRENCH: Sally-Anne.

SALLY-ANNE: I know, shut up Sally-Anne.

JILL MASTERSON: So, Trench - what are you going to do? A complete expos`e on the whole story? I suppose it will be quite a scoop for you?

STONEBRIDGE: I will make it worth your while - if you'll keep quite.

TRENCH: There is no cause to worry. As long as Mayflower Court remains, there is no need for me to say or do anything.

(Softer music changes the scene and time.)

(We hear TRENCH walking along the outside balcony-corridors of Mayflower Court.)

TRENCH: Ah, Mr. Jenkins, I'm glad I bumped into you. I have some wonderful news.

JENKINS: Excellent, so when are they sending the bulldozers in to finally flatten this useless pile of concrete? The sooner, the better. You can give me a date, can't you?

TRENCH: Oh yes, the date is only next month...

(We hear JENKINS rubbing his hands with glee.)

JENKINS: Earlier than I dared to hope...

TRENCH: ... when the Mayflower Refurbishment Project is due to begin.

JENKINS: *(Who says not quite believing:)* So, the flats are not going?

TRENCH: Mayflower Court is here to stay. Isn't that wonderful, ex-Sergeant Jenkins?

JENKINS: Err, yes - I suppose.

(A brief interlude of music moves things on a little bit.)

TRENCH: So, Old Tom, what do you think of this week's Stokeham Herald headline?

(OLD TOM opens up the newspaper.)

OLD TOM: 'The Mayflower Blossoms' ...very nice.

TRENCH: The headline was Sally-Anne's idea... unfortunately.

OLD TOM: 'Councilor Stonebridge has confirmed that the Mayflower Court flats are not only to remain, but to be fully refurbished and modernized - thanks to a campaign by the Stokeham Herald...' They will not be refurbishing anything in here. I like it just the way it is.

TRENCH: Now, Old Tom, why doesn't that surprise me?

(We hear OLD TOM fold the newspaper up and then throw it on the floor.)

TRENCH: By the way, I checked at the Station and Sergeant Strong confirmed that the inquiry, at the time of Jill's father's death was officially declared an accident, witnessed - along with Jenkins naturally - by the duty sergeant of the day and, surprisingly, the Chief Inspector. Something to do with a wet, slippery floor and a fall...

OLD TOM: A tragic accident? Simply far too convenient for Jill Masterson to ever believe…

TRENCH: But it seems that Jenkins was only guilty of greed…

OLD TOM: Strange that the Chief Inspector was there though… Unless he was there to dismiss Sergeant Jenkins as criminal allegations would have probably been building up against him by then.

TRENCH: Analytical deduction at its best… and I imagine you could be right.

OLD TOM: I am right… I think…

TRENCH: So, the Mayflower Mystery is finally over.

OLD TOM: You did quite well, my boy. You just required a little prodding in the right direction…

TRENCH: It's been fun though, hasn't it?

OLD TOM: Oh yes, I haven't had to think like this for a long, long time…

TRENCH: Tell me more.

OLD TOM: That was all in the past. I only concern myself with the present.

TRENCH: Good for you. Well, I don't think I'll be calling on the Armchair Detective again, though. Goodbye Old Tom.

OLD TOM: If you ever need my help on any other mysteries you may stumble over - you know where I am.

TRENCH: I know where you are.

(TRENCH gets up to leave.)

OLD TOM: Just before you go, Trench - would you pass me my cup of tea?

TRENCH: All right. Hey, wait a minute, there are two
cups here.

OLD TOM: Of course. One is for me... and one is for you.

TRENCH: But that's the first time you have offered me
anything.

OLD TOM: I know.

(We hear the slight clatter of crockery as the teas are passed.)

TRENCH: This tea is stone cold; do I have to drink it?

OLD TOM: It would be rude not to.

TRENCH: Here goes then... Ughh! This tea is dreadfully
cold... but curiously pleasant.

CLOSING MYSTERY MUSIC

THE ARMCHAIR DETECTIVE

and the

Manor-House Mystery

INTRODUCTION

A missing girl...

The manipulative aristocrat, Marcus Dreadbury.
A local gangster with a drug-dealing problem.
The Manor's locked room, with a dusty handle.
Stables, but with no sign of any horses.
A subterranean stream.
Marcus' madcap father.
And a Manor-House full of surprises.

Trench and Old Tom must somehow make the connection, if they are to succeed at playing find-the-lady...

Can I incorporate an old-fashioned manor-house mystery into The Armchair Detective *format? Yes – but I need the help of my favourite gangster, Sawn-Off to further muddy the waters, especially of the Dreadbury Punchbowl...*

CAST LIST

TRENCH

OLD TOM

SALLY-ANNE

EDITOR LAW

MARCUS DREADBURY

SAWN-OFF

LORD DEVESHAM

GEMMA

LANDLORD

HAPPY

ACT ONE

OPENING MYSTERY MUSIC

OLD TOM: I have not seen you for months, young Trench. And as you can see, Mayflower Court is still standing. How can I help?

TRENCH: Yes, it certainly is, Old Tom. I just thought I'd have a chat - that's all.

OLD TOM: I will ask you again: what's on your mind?

(TRENCH shuffles uncomfortably)

TRENCH: How's the armchair?

OLD TOM: As you can see, just as comfy as ever.

TRENCH: And the refurbishment project? Has the Mayflower had its makeover?

OLD TOM: Yes, the refurbishment project is complete.

TRENCH: Can't say I've noticed.

OLD TOM: Naturally I refused to let them in here. I like…

TRENCH: …it just the way it is - I know.

OLD TOM: If you've just come here to annoy me, Trench - then you are succeeding.

TRENCH: No, I'm sorry.

OLD TOM: Is it girlfriend trouble? Do you wish for my advice on the birds and the bees?

TRENCH: Not exactly, but it does concern Sally-Anne.

OLD TOM: Go on.

TRENCH: She has been dating this shifty so-called aristocrat by the name of Marcus Dreadbury. I just don't like him.

OLD TOM: *(Who laughs, softly.)* Accuse me of pointing out the obvious, but is all this fuelled by the green-eyed monster?

TRENCH: No, it's not that. Simply for Sally-Anne's safety, you understand, I did a background check on him.

OLD TOM: *(Who coughs.)* For your sake, I hope Sally-Anne doesn't find out about that.

TRENCH: Yes, I know what you mean, Old Tom.

OLD TOM: Well, young man - what did the background check reveal about this Marcus Dreadbury?

TRENCH: A previous girlfriend of his, a Miss Emmy Hargreaves disappeared whilst visiting Marcus at the Dreadbury family home. Apparently she's never been seen since.

OLD TOM: That's actually not much to go on - but I can see why you are concerned, Trench.

TRENCH: So, what do you suggest?

OLD TOM: Keep a close eye on your fellow reporter. Now, would you pass me my cup of tea?

TRENCH: Here.

OLD TOM: I would have made you one, but I didn't know you were coming.

(A short piece of music changes scene and time.)

(We hear TRENCH yawning.)

TRENCH: Another busy day at the hi-tech, modern offices of the dynamic Stokeham Herald. Hah.

SALLY-ANNE: Hmm, yes. We have had plenty of rain lately.

TRENCH: Oh Sally-Anne, didn't I tell you before? I fell down a manhole on the way to work, and this gigantic rat nearly…

SALLY-ANNE: Oh, lovely.

TRENCH: Anyway enough about Editor Law… Earth to Sally-Anne - are you receiving?

SALLY-ANNE: Sorry Trench. I was miles away.

TRENCH: More like on another planet.

SALLY-ANNE: I was just thinking…

TRENCH: About a mysterious aristocrat, by any chance?

SALLY-ANNE: My thoughts did just touch upon Marcus, yes. What do you mean 'mysterious'?

TRENCH: You don't know very much about him.

SALLY-ANNE: What do you want me to do - a background check or something?

TRENCH: *(Says guiltily:)* Of course not.

SALLY-ANNE: Anyhow, the Dreadbury Family can be traced back centuries - sixteenth, I think. So, how much do you want to know?

TRENCH: Me? I don't want to know anything - nothing to do with me.

SALLY-ANNE: Exactly.

TRENCH: Sixteenth century, eh? That's an awful long time to be lord of the manor.

SALLY-ANNE: Will you shut - oh hello Editor Law.

EDITOR LAW: Afternoon. What are you two young people doing this evening?

SALLY-ANNE: I will be spending the evening with Marcus. I think he's planning on taking me to that ridiculously expensive Italian restaurant...

TRENCH: And I'm washing my hair.

EDITOR LAW: Your plans have now changed. I want you both to investigate a story...

(We hear TRENCH trying to suppress a laugh.)

SALLY-ANNE: But sir, that's not fair.

TRENCH: Sounds perfectly fine to me.

SALLY-ANNE: Trench - shut up, will you?

EDITOR LAW: We have had several letters from the locals at the Cock and Pheasant Public House, claiming that the Landlord is regularly watering down his ale. I want you to look into it.

TRENCH: Oh yes - we could pose as normal punters; drinking plenty of beers; seemingly enjoying ourselves but all the time, watching...

EDITOR LAW: *(Who clears his throat.)* Yes, you'll probably have a barrel of laughs.

SALLY-ANNE: That was awful.

EDITOR LAW: I suppose it was - but just be there.

(We hear EDITOR LAW leave the office.)

TRENCH: I thought it was quite good - Editor Law doesn't often come out with funnies. Oh, come on Sally-Anne, what are you so miserable about?

SALLY-ANNE: I won't be able to see Marcus.

TRENCH: Yes you will - just invite him along to the Cock and Pheasant to join us.

SALLY-ANNE: Wonderful idea, Trench. Oh, sometimes I could kiss you!

TRENCH: Me and my big mouth.

(A few humorous notes move the scene to the evening.)

(We hear the pouring of a pint of Bitter by the LANDLORD and the usual sort of background of a pub - conversations etc.)

LANDLORD: Do you normally watch the pouring of your pint so enthusiastically?

TRENCH: I'm sorry Landlord - bad habit I suppose. It is just that I believe that pouring a pint is really an art form.

LANDLORD: Oh, you do? That's all right then. There's your perfect pint and a Pimms and lemonade.

TRENCH: Thanks.

(We hear the exchange of money. TRENCH moves a chair before eventually settling next to SALLY-ANNE.)

TRENCH: Cheers.

SALLY-ANNE: Hmm.

TRENCH: What's wrong with you, Sally-Anne? Afraid that lover-boy won't lower himself to turn up in this fine old establishment?

SALLY-ANNE: Marcus has given his word - so he will be here, yes even here, in the Cock an' Pheasant.

TRENCH: You have faith in this Marcus, then?

SALLY-ANNE: Oh, stop being ridiculous Trench - I've only just arrived. How long have you been here?

TRENCH: About an hour.

SALLY-ANNE: And what have you discovered, apart from the various merits of the many lagers and bitters?

TRENCH: Hah, well the Landlord is definitely a sneaky character who doesn't like being watched - but it was just before I set foot in this pub where I overheard a rather interesting conversation.

SALLY-ANNE: Like when the price of crisps are going up next?

(We hear SALLY-ANNE heavy breathe a 'get on with it then, will you?')

TRENCH: It seems that this 'watering down' lark is big business.

That unpleasant, 'you don't want to know' type - a local 'business man' known as Sawn-Off was politely threatening the Landlord. Sawn-off as in Shotgun.

SALLY-ANNE: 'Sawn-off' not him. He doesn't usually use his surname, 'Shotgun'. Were his bunch of heavies with him?

TRENCH: Probably. They are obviously in on this low-alcohol beer racket.

SALLY-ANNE: *(Cuts in.)* Better for one's health though

TRENCH: *(Continues.)* And I think they were in the process of extracting their cut.

SALLY-ANNE: We should tread very carefully with this story.

TRENCH: I know, I like my face exactly where it is.

            (*TRENCH takes another sip of his beer*.)

SALLY-ANNE: *(Says loudly:)* Oh Marcus - over here darling.

            (Chairs are shuffled as TRENCH and SALLY-ANNE stand up.)

MARCUS: *(His voice is deep and sickly.)* Dear, Sally-Anne - and Trench I presume.

TRENCH: Hello, err sir, Lord..?

MARCUS: As dear old Daddy is still alive, I have yet to inherit my hereditary title so, Marcus will suffice.

TRENCH: ...Marcus.

MARCUS: *(Who clicks his fingers.)* A pint of your best bitter, barman and whatever my young friends are drinking. Bring them over.

            (We just hear the LANDLORD grumble a 'yes' and a

'who does he think he is?' to his nearest customer. There was a low rumble of laughter at 'bring them over'.)

        (We hear them sit down.)

MARCUS: The lady is beautiful, Trench. Is she not?

TRENCH: Who are you talking about?

        (SALLY-ANNE kicks TRENCH under the table.)

TRENCH: Ouch.

SALLY-ANNE: Ignore him, Marcus. I am so glad you came. We are on rather a dull assignment.

MARCUS: I admit, I usually frequent more grandiose locations.

        (The LANDLORD places the drinks on the table.)

MARCUS: One will settle the bill at close of evening.

LANDLORD: Yes 'one' will. *(Gruffly, he returns to the bar.)*

        (MARCUS drinks some of his pint.)

MARCUS: A rather peculiar taste. Now, what is the nature of your assignment?

TRENCH: Oh, I wouldn't do you the disservice of boring you with the details.

MARCUS: As you wish.

TRENCH: Oh, it's just so lovely to see such a handsome couple together.

SALLY-ANNE: *(Says in a warning tone:)* Trench.

MARCUS: Yes - and, dearest Sally-Anne, I wish us to be together this weekend for shooting at Dreadbury Manor.

TRENCH: *(Who coughs)* No, she err can't.

MARCUS: Why ever not? Prey the lady speaks for herself.

SALLY-ANNE: I would love to come. Thank-you Marcus. Now, Trench, why can't I?

TRENCH: Editor Law might have another assignment for us.

SALLY-ANNE: Yes well, he may own my evenings but not my weekends. I'll be there, Marcus.

TRENCH: Shooting you said? I've always wanted to do that. Ah well...

MARCUS: Then you must come too, dear Trench.

TRENCH: Good-oh.

MARCUS: Look for the line of oaks that line my estate...

SALLY-ANNE: Wonderful - excuse me a minute. *(She leaves.)*

MARCUS: Never been shooting? Try to be very careful though, there can be the most dreadful accidents...

              (Ominous music changes the time and scene to the following day.)

OLD TOM: So, you will be shooting Grouse, my boy?

TRENCH: Yes, not really my idea of fun, but I couldn't let Sally-Anne go on her own, could I?

OLD TOM: Evidently not.

TRENCH: Then, you will never guess what happened next in the pub?

OLD TOM: Sawn-Off and his heavies arrived and Marcus put his aristocratic arms around young Sally-Anne?

TRENCH: I'm speechless. Sometimes, Old Tom, you amaze me.

OLD TOM: Only sometimes, Trench?

TRENCH: You are going to tell me how you came up with that astonishing deduction?

OLD TOM: You had excitedly mentioned Sawn-Off earlier. Your challenge was made in exactly the same tones. Then, assuming my deduction was correct and Sawn-Off had entered the scene, it is easy to presume a gentleman would hold his girl protectively, knowing the mobster's reputation, say like a mother goose protecting her goslings under her wings - if that was what Marcus was actually doing of course.

TRENCH: Thanks for not saying, 'elementary, my dear Trench.'

OLD TOM: I was sorely tempted.

TRENCH: And before you tell me, Sawn-Off had a chat with the Landlord who seemed to lose all colour in his face...

OLD TOM: Which is completely consistent with their character traits.

TRENCH: But the weirdest thing was 'the look'.

OLD TOM: Define 'the look'. And to whom was 'the look' intended?

TRENCH: 'The look' was predictably threatening, but there was something else - like an intense questioning, a strange sense of curiosity, if you like. Sawn-Off seemed to be staring at Marcus...

OLD TOM: Very interesting...

(OLD TOM coughs very badly.)

TRENCH: Here, let me fetch you some water.

OLD TOM: No, no - never touch the stuff.

TRENCH: I give up.

OLD TOM: So, are you going to tell me about your trip to the Police Station this morning? And before you look open-mouthed again, they're several Police-headed reports sticking out of your briefcase.

TRENCH: Yes, unofficially and in complete confidence Sergeant Strong let me have them for research.

OLD TOM: Concerning the missing Emmy Hargreaves, no doubt?

TRENCH: Correct.

OLD TOM: You'll have obviously read them by now and probably have to return them very soon so you might as well save me the bother and give me the edited highlights.

TRENCH: Marcus was not only seeing Emmy, they were engaged to be married. Emmy spent her last weekend at the Dreadbury Manor-House with Marcus, naturally, and his father, Lord Devesham-Dreadbury for a spot of shooting. Now, can you see why I'm worried?

OLD TOM: Lightning never strikes twice, young Trench but then again, history does have an unpleasant habit of repeating itself.

TRENCH: Also, Miss Emmy Hargreaves was rumoured to be in the employ of a certain Sawn-Off and his merry band of men known as the Syndicate...

OLD TOM: That, I didn't expect. What was Emmy's connection to the low-life of Stokeham and district?

TRENCH: Sergeant Strong stressed it was only a rumour, but the whispers from mostly unreliable sources, did mention Drugs. I don't know more than that.

OLD TOM: But that tells us an awful lot.

TRENCH: That Sawn-Off saw off Emmy? That she died an addict's death, if indeed she was an addict? Or is Marcus Dreadbury somehow involved in her disappearance or even murder?

OLD TOM: Searching questions, Trench. Very old families like the Dreadburys usually have plenty of skeletons in their cupboard.

TRENCH: And my visit to Dreadbury Manor this weekend will be the perfect opportunity to start opening some cupboards...

OLD TOM: In the meantime, my boy - nip into the kitchen and make us both a cup of tea.

TRENCH: But you usually have it made.

OLD TOM: So therefore it's your turn. Come on, tea doesn't make itself.

TRENCH: *(Says in the kitchen to himself.)* And besides, that would involve you getting up from that armchair of yours...

(A longer piece of mystery music indicates the end of Act One.)

ACT TWO

(We hear TRENCH walking along the streets of Stokeham.)

TRENCH: *(Whistling to himself.)* A hunting we will go…

                    (TRENCH suddenly stops walking.)

TRENCH: Excuse me sir, you happen to be blocking my way. If you wouldn't mind…

THUG: Move.

TRENCH: I was moving until you stopped me.

THUG: Over there.

TRENCH: I love these mono-syllabic types. You want me to move into that dark alleyway? Now, why didn't you say so?

(TRENCH is 'escorted' into the alleyway.)

TRENCH: I think that kind-hearted gentleman wants me to have a chat with you.

SAWN-OFF: You mean, 'Happy'.

TRENCH: He looks so miserable though.

(HAPPY grunts menacingly.)

TRENCH: No offence

SAWN-OFF: He is happy being miserable. Now, do you know who I am?

TRENCH: Only by reputation. You are a local gangst... I mean 'business man' whose trade name is, Sawn-Off.

SAWN-OFF: You have the advantage over me, what is yours?

TRENCH: I do not own a business, Mr Sawn-Off.

SAWN-OFF: (Says threateningly:) Name?

TRENCH: Trench. Pleased to meet you.

SAWN-OFF: Do not act the fool with me Trench, the last person who did laughed himself into an early grave. Do you follow me?

TRENCH: My understanding of your message, Sawn-Off is clear. Crystal.

SAWN-OFF: You were seen with a gentleman, a Marcus Dreadbury. Explain.

TRENCH: Oh relax, I don't really know this Marcus. I'm just a friend of a friend, that's all.

SAWN-OFF: Do you know his girlfriend?

TRENCH: Which one? He was going out with - now what was her name? She was an absolute award of a girl - that's it; her name is Emmy, Emmy Hargreaves. Now, I wonder where she has disappeared to?

(HAPPY smacks his fist into his palm.)

HAPPY: Boss..?

SAWN-OFF: No, not yet. Despite being a fool Trench, you amuse me. In fact I will carry on laughing till you have an unhappy accident.

TRENCH: How do you know I'm going to have an accident?

SAWN-OFF: They can be arranged. And for your sake, I hope you know nothing about dear Emmy.

HAPPY: (Who laughs.) Good one, 'arranged'. Hah.

SAWN-OFF: Laugh Trench.

TRENCH: Oh hilarious, Sawn-Off. Hah, hah.

(Music moves scene and time on.)

(We hear the car driving through the country lanes.)

TRENCH: I think we must be lost, Sally-Anne. There's no sign of Dreadbury Manor anywhere. Here, check the map.

(We hear SALLY-ANNE unfold the map.)

SALLY-ANNE: I can't make head nor tail of this.

TRENCH: Here, try reading it the right way up.

                     (TRENCH snatches the map, turns it the right way round and hands it back to SALLY-ANNE.)

SALLY-ANNE: I knew that, of course - I was just teasing.

TRENCH: Hah. Well, can you make out where we are?

SALLY-ANNE: Not really, Trench - we could do with one of those 'You Are Here' signs.

                     (TRENCH sighs heavily with evident frustration.)

SALLY-ANNE: We should have found it by now. Even though we're deep into the countryside, Marcus said it was only half-an-hour's drive from Stokeham.

TRENCH: And we've been driving for nearly an hour. Well, I suppose if we're going to be lost, it's best to be lost in beautiful scenery. There's the Great Southern Lake somewhere nearby and I mean, look at that majestic line of oak trees over there.

SALLY-ANNE: That's it Trench! Marcus told me there is a mall of oak trees leading to his estate.

TRENCH: *(Who takes a deep breath to calm himself.)*
Yes, yes he did.

TRENCH: Don't you mean his father's estate?

SALLY-ANNE: That's what I meant.

TRENCH: At least we've finally found this mystery manor, anyway.

SALLY-ANNE: 'Mystery' ah yes. Can you explain to me why you decided to join us on this weekend?

TRENCH: As I've already said, I fancied a spot of shooting.

SALLY-ANNE: Rubbish! You've always hated blood sports.

TRENCH: All right, alone with a stranger in a sprawling mansion. I was concerned for you Sally-Anne, that's all.

SALLY-ANNE: Well, I can look after myself.

(We hear the car stop.)

TRENCH: The grand Dreadbury gates. Hadn't you better pop out dear, and ring the bell or something?

SALLY-ANNE: I think dear Marcus will be more sophisticated than that. Look at that security camera up there. He's probably recognized us by now.

TRENCH: And if he doesn't?

SALLY-ANNE: I'd better pop out and ring the bell!

TRENCH: It looks like dear old Marcus has spotted us.
The gates are...

SALLY-ANNE: ...opening by remote control.

(We hear the gates opening.)

SALLY-ANNE: What are you waiting for Trenchy, drive on!

TRENCH: It is wise to hesitate before entering the lion's den.

(The car drives through the gates and ominous yet regal music changes the scene.)

SALLY-ANNE: Oh Marcus, this is truly a wondrous home. An oak-paneled library; classical dining hall; imposing portraits adorning the walls and this Drawing Room... exquisite.

MARCUS: I'm glad you like it, my dearest Sally. Would you care to offer an opinion on my humble abode, Trench?

TRENCH: Well, if you think having seventeen rooms in your abode is humble, I'd hate to see you when you're being arrogant.

SALLY-ANNE: (Who whispers sternly:) I'm warning you, Trench - behave.

TRENCH: Sorry Marcus, no offence intended.

MARCUS: I humbly accept your apology, old boy. And yes, I suppose you would hate to see me when I'm being arrogant.

SALLY-ANNE: I think this weekend will be marvelous, Marcus. We'll be all alone in this big house.

TRENCH: Wait a minute, why are you looking at me? Oh, don't worry - you'll hardly notice I'm here.

          (There is a knock on the door and it opens.)

MARCUS: Ah, Gemma, you've brought afternoon tea. Splendid.

GEMMA: My lord. Oh, I forgot the milk - I'll just go back for it.

MARCUS: Err... that's Gemma, the maid

TRENCH: So that's why she was wearing that outfit!

SALLY-ANNE: (Who again, sharply whispers to TRENCH.) Very funny, Trench - now stop it.

          (A fit of coughing and increasingly loud

footsteps are heard upstairs.)

MARCUS: Oh and my father Lord Devesham-Dreadbury is pottering around somewhere too.

SALLY-ANNE: I think we'd have more chance of being alone in Piccadilly Circus!

MARCUS: I assure you my sweet Sally-Anne, we will spend time alone.

TRENCH: Now that's what worries me.

MARCUS: Speak up Trench, I didn't quite catch that.

TRENCH: Sorry Marcus, I was just saying that all this lovey-dovey stuff reminds me of my previous girlfriend.

SALLY-ANNE: Oh dear, what are you talking about?

(We hear the door open.)

GEMMA: Panic over, I've found the milk.

TRENCH: It was so sad, you see - we were engaged to be married, and then poor Emma simply vanished off the face of the earth.

(There is an almighty crash as the maid, GEMMA drops the milk jug.)

GEMMA: Oh, sorry.

MARCUS: A fascinating story, Trench. I do expect to enjoy our shoot tomorrow…

(Ominous music changes the scene.)

SALLY-ANNE: Such a magnificent roaring fire, Trench. Now that's what I call a grand fireplace.

TRENCH: I know, it's almost big enough to walk through - if you happened to be made of asbestos or something.

SALLY-ANNE: Anyway, what was all that nonsense about Emma? I'm pretty sure you've never been out with an Emma before. And you've not even been engaged - to anyone.

TRENCH: Well, Sally-Anne, you see...

(We can just hear MARCUS and the maid's voice coming from a nearby room.)

SALLY-ANNE: Hang on, what's Marcus doing in the kitchen with the maid?

TRENCH: Why don't you go and find out?

SALLY-ANNE: I will.

(We hear SALLY-ANNE walk away but can still hear their voices.)

SALLY-ANNE: What's going on, Marcus?

MARCUS: Oh, I was just explaining to Gemma here my choices for evening dinner. You are in for a treat my dear, Sally-Anne.

SALLY-ANNE: Oh, that's all right then, Marcus - my Marcus.

GEMMA: Excuse me, my lord.

(The door is closed and TRENCH hears no more.)

TRENCH: I think I'll pour myself a drink - ah, sherry.

(We hear the clink of the decanter as TRENCH pours himself a sherry. At that moment, another door opens and Lord

DEVESHAM -Dreadbury arrives.)

DEVESHAM: I wouldn't drink, if I was you old boy.

TRENCH: Why ever not? Lord Devesham, I presume.
Trench, at your service.

DEVESHAM: Ah, Tiger Trench - you're next in to bat. Keep a
clear head, at least that's what Winnie always says.

TRENCH: I thought we were going shooting.

DEVESHAM: That's tomorrow. Today we're in the Pavilion
at Lords and about to thrash the West Indies.

TRENCH: Oh, I see - no I don't.

DEVESHAM: You're not even kitted out yet. Have you gone
mad?

TRENCH: I think one of us has.

DEVESHAM: Look lively Tiger. Beware of the demon
bowler. And as a special surprise, Lady Devesham, that's err Winnie to
you, is providing refreshments for afternoon tea.

TRENCH: Splendid, I'll… I'll just go and get kitted out
then.

                 *(TRENCH hastily leaves the room, closing the
door firmly behind him.)*

TRENCH: Oh, Gemma - have you seen Sally-Anne
anywhere?

GEMMA: I believe she is out walking with Marcus.

TRENCH: Oh no - I mean I'll go and quickly catch up with
them.

(Faster-paced music changes the scene.)

(We hear TRENCH's footsteps as he runs across the gravel path/driveway. He then runs through the woods, his panic over SALLY-ANNE's safety increasing - the music reflects this.)

TRENCH: *(Who shouts:)* Marcus! *(TRENCH breathlessly adds:)* What are you doing staring at the swamp?

MARCUS: Staring... thinking... *(He snaps out of it.)* Swamp? I assume you are referring to the Dreadbury Punchbowl.

TRENCH: Dreadbury Punchbowl? What an odd name for a swamp.

MARCUS: It is thus named because there is a subterranean stream that flows through to the Great Southern Lake, a few miles away - hence the bubbles - here look.

(We can hear the bubbling.)

TRENCH: How err unsettling.

MARCUS: I agree Trench. It always reminds me of someone drowning, struggling to draw their last breath...

TRENCH: Where is Sally-Anne?

MARCUS: Evidently not here.

TRENCH: What have you done with her?

MARCUS: I detect a note of panic in your voice, why?

TRENCH: Just tell me where she is. The maid said you both went out walking.

MARCUS: Oh yes, we did. If you must know, my dear, sweet Sally-Anne has gone to powder her nose. You know how women do that sort of thing.

TRENCH: Is that all?

                        (TRENCH slowly walks up to MARCUS,
evidently relaxing a little.)

TRENCH: I didn't realize that your mother, Marcus, was
still alive.

MARCUS: I'm afraid not, my mother Lady Winnifred died
a long time ago.

TRENCH: But…

MARCUS: You must have been chatting with father.
Allow me to explain, mother passed away whilst at Lord's cricket
ground watching a Test match against the West Indies. Father has
never basically recovered from it. He believes his 'Winnie' is still alive
and life is one perpetual game of cricket.

TRENCH: I know a few people like that!

MARCUS: However, the worst thing is…

TRENCH: Yes..?

MARCUS: To rub salt into the wounds, those West Indies
blighters won the match!

TRENCH: How awful. Oh, on the way here I couldn't
help but notice the stables.

MARCUS: How terribly observant of you.

TRENCH: Thing is, there wasn't any horses there – not a
single one.

MARCUS: There are no gee gees at Dreadbury.

TRENCH: Quite. Well perhaps, Sally-Anne has finished powdering her nose by now.

MARCUS: Perhaps she has. You go to her, Trench. I must go and check that the shotguns are in order for tomorrow's shooting.

TRENCH: Right, then.

MARCUS: After all, we wouldn't want any accidents, would we?

(More heavy notes emphasizing the threat and a longer piece of music moves things on to the following day.)

SALLY-ANNE: What a wonderful meal, or should I say banquet, we had last night.

TRENCH: I know Sall'. Duck soup, roast pheasant and I don't think I could eat another Quale's egg.

SALLY-ANNE: The meal was that heavy, it kept me up half the night.

TRENCH: Yes, I remember.

SALLY-ANNE: Mmm, what a lovely smell: sausages, bacon, eggs...

TRENCH: Yes, the maid must be cooking a full English breakfast.

SALLY-ANNE: I'll just go and pour some juice, coming?

TRENCH: Give me a moment, then I'll join you.

(We hear SALLY-ANNE leave the room.)

TRENCH: What I really could do with now is a chat with Old Tom.

(At that moment, the telephone rings, TRENCH

tentatively answers it.)

TRENCH: Hello.

OLD TOM: Good morning, young Trench.

TRENCH: Old Tom! But how could you possibly..?

OLD TOM: It may surprise you to know, I am just about capable of using a telephone directory.

TRENCH: I've so much to tell you, Old Tom. Where should I start?

OLD TOM: I've always found the beginning a useful place...

TRENCH: No I won't, I'll first tell you what happened in the middle of the night.

OLD TOM: Wait a minute, would you pass me my cup of tea? Oh sorry, of course you can't. I will have to struggle myself.

                           (We hear OLD TOM struggle to reach his tea.)

OLD TOM: Ah, that's better. Tear on, Trench.

TRENCH: Well I woke up looking for the bathroom and bumped into Sally-Anne who was doing the same. We tried the nearest door but it was locked. This woke Marcus up and he seemed annoyed. He dismissed the locked room as private and simply not in use. He as good as told Sally-Anne it was none of her business when she suggested taking a 'peek'.

OLD TOM: There is nothing more mysterious than a locked room in a manor-house...

TRENCH: Could poor Emmy Hargreaves be held prisoner in there? Assuming she is still alive.

OLD TOM: You have something else, in particular, to tell me.

TRENCH: Yes I do, but how did you know? Never mind - as I returned to my bedroom I left the door slightly ajar and could just make out a whispered conversation between Sally-Anne and Marcus.

OLD TOM: And..?

TRENCH: Shockingly, Sally-Anne suggested that she could slip into Marcus' bedroom. I tell you, I didn't know what to do.

OLD TOM; But no action was necessary, as master Marcus said - that they should know each other rather more before making that next step, err shall we say.

TRENCH: Now, come on Old Tom - you couldn't have known that.

OLD TOM: I can read, err situations.

TRENCH: But the bottom line is - do you think Sally-Anne is in danger?

OLD TOM: I believe that is a likely possibility, but I still need to know more.

(We hear someone enter the room.)

SALLY-ANNE: What do you mean 'is Sally-Anne in danger?' Who are you speaking to, Trench?

TRENCH: Just having a chat with Old Tom, that's all.

SALLY-ANNE: Give me that 'phone. *(We hear SALLY-ANNE snatch the 'phone off TRENCH.)* Hello good Old Tom, hello..? Who were you speaking to? The line's dead.

TRENCH: Yes, and so might you be - if we don't get out of here.

(A longer piece of mystery music indicates the end of Act Two.)

ACT THREE

(We hear a few shots as TRENCH and MARCUS try to kill their prey.)

MARCUS: You missed, Trench.

TRENCH: So did you, Marcus.

MARCUS: Not exactly, I was firing a few warning shots to manipulate my prey.

TRENCH: Good excuse, I mean reason. Who's letting the birds out - the gamekeeper?

MARCUS: No, a game keeper is not necessary. The Dreadbury Estate is famous for its generous stock of Grouse. Controlled shooting of said pheasants here, dates back centuries.

TRENCH: Missed the blighter again, although as they say I managed to ruffle a few feathers. Err, wait a minute, Marcus - you seem to be pointing your shotgun straight at me, why?

MARCUS: Always so many questions, Trench - may I ask you one?

TRENCH: Fire away - except don't. Ask away to your heart's content though.

MARCUS: If you really want to know about Emmy Hargreaves, why don't you just ask - you know, another one of your questions?

TRENCH: All right, I will. What has happened to her? Where is Emmy Hargreaves? And how do you know I'm looking for her?

                           (We hear a click as MARCUS prepares to fire.)

MARCUS: Your none too subtle slip about looking for your own supposed Emma was a trifle obvious.

TRENCH: Yes, I admit that was a bit crass. You can stop pointing that gun at me, if you like.

MARCUS: As you are probably aware, Emmy and I were engaged, however for reasons only known to her - maybe the pressure of it all, or she went off me - I don't know, she decided to leave suddenly, not even having the good grace to leave a note. You do believe me, don't you?

TRENCH: Of course I do. I believe you, absolutely.

                           (MARCUS' shot rings out.)

TRENCH: Ouch! That bullet singed my ear!

MARCUS: But killed the Grouse that was moving just behind your head. I venture that tonight's culinary delights will be entirely predictable.

TRENCH: You win, Marcus.

MARCUS: I invariably do. We should return to Dreadbury Manor.

TRENCH: One more thing, though - did you and Emmy go on plenty of extravagant parties?

MARCUS: Yes we did, actually - but why ask?

TRENCH: Sorry, just another of my insufferable questions.

(Thoughtful music shifts the scene once more.)

SALLY-ANNE: Right, while we're alone, Trench - I want to know why my life is in such supposed peril and what are you actually doing here?

TRENCH: All right, I'll tell you - wait, I think Marcus is coming.

(We hear the door open.)

TRENCH: Ah, Lord Devesham, delighted.

(TRENCH groans.)

DEVESHAM: We are forty runs behind, Tiger Trench. A quick half-century from you and we'll stuff the blighters! Oh, apologies Miss - I did not realize there's a lady present, as I'm always saying to my dearest Winnie...

TRENCH: Mad as a hatter.

SALLY-ANNE: Apology accepted, sir. *(SALLY-ANNE suddenly takes a deep breath.)* Marcus!

MARCUS: I'm sure Sally-Anne would prefer to watch the match than talk about it, father.

DEVESHAM: Oh dear, another one of our chaps out. You're on next, Trench!

MARCUS: How about we all relax for a while in the err Pavilion first - and drink some punch.

                        (MARCUS rings for the Maid, who enters.)

GEMMA: You rang, my lord.

SALLY-ANNE: It's not fair, I've always wanted to say that!

MARCUS: Gemma, would you be so kind as to fetch our silver bowl? We shall all be partaking in punch.

TRENCH: Hmm, I think you are trying to give me a clue, Marcus.

SALLY-ANNE: Oh dear Trench, what are you talking about?

TRENCH: Punch… bowl… the Dreadbury Punchbowl! Excuse me, I'm just going out for a walk.

                        (TRENCH shuts the door sharply behind him.)

DEVESHAM: *(Who shouts.)* Knock 'em for six, Tiger!

                        (Pacey music plays as TRENCH runs along the gravel path and through the woods until he reaches the swamp.)

TRENCH: The Dreadbury Punchbowl…

SAWN-OFF: Trench, what are you doing staring at that swamp?

TRENCH: That's funny, that's the same question I asked Marcus… Sawn-Off! What are you doing here?

SAWN-OFF: I am here to find-the-lady namely Emmy Hargreaves. Where is she?

TRENCH: I wish I knew. Why do you want her?

SAWN-OFF: The Syndicate want her back. No one ever leaves the Syndicate... I made her into a Lady and she was our window to the aristocracy. She did extremely well. She sold many drugs for us, at highly lucrative prices.

TRENCH: Which she sold at the many parties her and Marcus frequented, I see. Come to think of it, I don't really know what the lady looked like. Enlighten me, Sawn-Off.

SAWN-OFF: Platinum blonde - and she was beautiful in a regal sort of way.

TRENCH: Well, the only girls here are Sally-Anne who is dark haired and the Maid is a brunette. Neither of them are particularly regal... Wait a minute, what's that in the swamp, by the bushes?

SAWN-OFF: A body?

TRENCH: If I can reach, I'll get it with this branch.

          (We hear rustling as TRENCH hauls it out of the swamp with a long branch.)

TRENCH: I'm afraid not, it's just a coat.

SAWN-OFF: But it's Emmy's coat, I recognize it. I must bring Happy and my associates down to dredge this swamp - the body must be somewhere.

TRENCH: See the bubbles, Sawn-Off - that's where some sort of underground river emerges which originates from the Great Southern Lake - which is where the body of poor Miss Hargreaves has probably been swept to, by the currents. And that lake is far too big to be dredged up, even by your heavies. *(TRENCH takes a deep breath.)* The Lady in the Lake...

SAWN-OFF: I'm sorry, she is dead?

TRENCH: Why, do you miss her?

SAWN-OFF: No, I wanted to kill her myself – at least the horses didn't though.

TRENCH: Say what?

SAWN-OFF: She was allergic to horses, didn't you know? Obviously not. See you around, Trench.

TRENCH: Give my regards to Happy.

(More music and a change of scene.)

TRENCH: I'll sneak back through the kitchen. *(He has a sharp intake of breath.)* Marcus and the Maid are embracing - and kissing! I must tell Sally-Anne.

(TRENCH sneaks through to the Drawing Room.)

TRENCH: Sally-Anne, where are you?

(His only answer is the 'phone ringing.)

TRENCH: Hello? Old Tom... I've so much more to tell you.

(Music passes some time.)

TRENCH: So, what do you deduce?

OLD TOM: As far as I'm concerned, the case is almost closed. I could explain the mystery of the missing society girl, come drug pusher right now - but I won't. This is a case I want you to crack. Now, how do you propose to gain access to the locked room? Come on think, Trench, think.

TRENCH: I don't know. Marcus said the bedroom is unused but I was sure I heard something… The door is not used though - there was dust on the handle. My hand was covered in it.

OLD TOM: Then the secret must be literally staring you in the face.

TRENCH: I can only see the fireplace. Of course, I said to Sally-Anne it was almost big enough to walk through.

OLD TOM: And, young Trench, these old manor-houses are notorious for secret passageways - so venture forth, walk through and solve the mystery.

(The 'phone goes dead and TRENCH replaces the receiver.)

TRENCH: Sally-Anne!

SALLY-ANNE: You're obviously back, Trench - now tell me what's going on.

TRENCH: *(Who takes a deep breath.)* I believe that Marcus Dreadbury's previous girlfriend, err fiancé Emmy Hargreaves has been murdered by Marcus. He may have disposed the body in the Dreadbury Punchbowl - that's a swamp leading to the Great Lake, or she's imprisoned in that locked room upstairs. Want to find out?

SALLY-ANNE: Might as well, I suppose. I've nothing else to do at the moment. I think you've finally flipped though, Trench.

TRENCH: The fire has long since died, so let's walk through it.

(We hear them walk through the remains of the fire.)

SALLY-ANNE: A secret passageway with a twisting, spiral staircase.

(They walk up the heavy stone steps.)

TRENCH: Oh, and Marcus is having a fling with his maid.

SALLY-ANNE: What!? I'll kill him.

TRENCH: Not if he kills you first. *(We hear the creepy sound of a rocking chair.)* There's a rocking chair, rocking.

SALLY-ANNE There's someone on the chair. *(She screams.)* A skeleton!

TRENCH: Not so much a skeleton in the cupboard - this one resides in a whole bedroom!

(We hear the key tumble in the lock and the door creaks open.)

TRENCH: Marcus, is that what's left of poor Emmy?

MARCUS: I think we should all return to the Drawing Room, sit down, drink some Punch and talk about this in a civilized fashion.

(Solemnly yet surprisingly they do as Marcus requests and walk downstairs.)

TRENCH: I prefer to stand, actually.

SALLY-ANNE: Me too.

MARCUS: As you wish. Oh, hello father.

DEVESHAM: Would you believe it, my boy? Some blighter's left your mother's door open. Winnie will catch her death. See you all in the Pavilion. Cheers!

(We hear DEVESHAM leave the room.)

MARCUS: Now where were we? Now as you have probably gathered, the skeleton upstairs is the remains of my late mother. It pleases father and I don't really care what you or anyone else thinks.

SALLY-ANNE: What about this Emmy Hargreaves, Marcus? Have you, have you..?

MARCUS: Murdered her? *(He rings the bell and the door opens.)*

GEMMA: You rang?

MARCUS: For Gemma, read Emmy. Remove your wig, my dearest.

(GEMMA removes her wig.)

TRENCH: Platinum blonde!

SALLY-ANNE: I think you owe us - me an explanation.

MARCUS: I am truly sorry my sweet, Sally-Anne - but you were little more than a diversion. I first met Emmy at a society party - the type of venue I later discovered, where she pedaled those dreadful drugs of hers. We fell in love, of course, but Emmy was trapped.

GEMMA: Sawn-Off and his Syndicate would not let me leave the Drug dealing - it was too valuable. They wouldn't even accept Marcus' money, something to do with their reputation. In fact the only way I could be free of them and be with Marcus was to...

MARCUS: ... die - or disappear.

TRENCH: Or both - which is why you left Emmy's coat in the swamp, err the Dreadbury Punchbowl.

SALLY-ANNE: And that's why you were courting me Marcus, so obviously - putting your arm around me when Sawn-Off turned up in the Cock and Pheasant to at least make it look like you were over Emmy here.

TRENCH: And to confirm you had finally accepted your fiancé's disappearance.

MARCUS: I am sorry you were both drawn into this.

GEMMA: Me too, we are in love - that's all.

SALLY-ANNE: But I did have feelings for you, Marcus - so you deserve this.

(SALLY-ANNE slaps MARCUS across the face.)

TRENCH: Well, thanks for a truly wonderful weekend! Come on, Sally-Anne, I really think we must be going.

(A slightly longer piece of reflective music changes the scene and pace.)

TRENCH: A pint of Bitter please - Sally-Anne, what are you doing behind the Bar?

SALLY-ANNE: A girl has to make money where she can, these days - even if it's toiling away in the Cock and Pheasant.

TRENCH: You toil beautifully - it suits you!

SALLY-ANNE: Thanks, Trench - I'm working here undercover, actually.

TRENCH: And what have you uncovered?

SALLY-ANNE: I have retrieved evidence from the Landlord's Ledger which will blow this diluting beer scam right open.

TRENCH: A word of warning, Sally-Anne - it's quite possible you may upset Sawn-Off and his Syndicate. Believe it or not, I like your pretty little neck the way it is.

SALLY-ANNE: Don't you dare patronize...

TRENCH: Shh, the Landlord's coming and we have
visitors.

                         (We hear activity as two men enter the pub.)

LANDLORD: What can I get you, gentlemen? On the house,
of course.

SAWN-OFF: The usual.

TRENCH: Sawn-Off and Happy, delighted to bump into
you again. Are you here for social or business reasons?

HAPPY: Here.. Collect.

SAWN-OFF: No, Happy - how many times have I told you?
We don't ever collect, we are simply paid for services rendered.

HAPPY: Sorry... Sawn-Off.

SAWN-OFF: I'm sure I'll manage to somehow forgive you
in the fullness of time. And what is your business here, Trench? Wait,
that barmaid seems vaguely familiar. Drat, she's gone in the back.

TRENCH: Don't they all look the same, Sawn-Off?

SAWN-OFF: What, barmaids?

TRENCH: Err, yes.

SAWN-OFF: Actually Trench, I am glad we've met again,
after that ill-fated search for our Drug Dealer. I now consider you a
friend and I like the way you operate.

TRENCH: Gee, thanks.

SAWN-OFF: My brother, who let us say, runs a business enterprise in the East-End of London has met with an unfortunate and fatal accident - which means I will be taking over his patch, along with Happy and the rest of the Syndicate, of course. Care to join us, as my right-hand man?

HAPPY: Me right man.

SAWN-OFF: Sorry Happy is right. As my left-hand man then?

TRENCH: A tempting offer, but if I wanted to eventually leave the, err Syndicate I would hate for you to have to go through all that rigmarole like you did with Miss Hargreaves. And, anyway - I'm just a pen-pusher at heart.

HAPPY: Me kill... boss?

SAWN-OFF: No, not today Happy. I've already told you that Trench is now a friend of mine - and we don't kill friends, do we? Well, not usually.

HAPPY: Me happy.

SAWN-OFF: Yes, I know. Now Happy follow - I have some concluding business with the Landlord. Goodbye for now, Trench.

TRENCH: Be seeing you.

(We hear them move away.)

SALLY-ANNE: Good, they've gone.

TRENCH: And we don't need to worry about them, because Sawn-Off and Co. are off to London.

SALLY-ANNE: That's a relief.

TRENCH: Sally-Anne, Marcus really hurt you, didn't he? I'm sorry it worked out the way it did.

SALLY-ANNE: I'm not, because after all, I'm glad I didn't disappear!

(Music moves time along and the scene changes.)

TRENCH: So, Old Tom before I've really even said anything, you've told me the complete story of the mayhem at the manor-house, how?

OLD TOM: Deductions enlighten many a shadowy corner. Firstly having deduced where and who Emmy really was, it was easy to assume that the locked bedroom had more to do with the eccentric delusions of Devesham rather than his son. However, the lady in the lake argument was more compelling.

TRENCH: Yes, how did you know there never was a body in the Dreadbury Punchbowl.

OLD TOM: It was all too contrived, Trench.

TRENCH: All right, how did Marcus know I would even meet up with Sawn-Off by the swamp?

OLD TOM: You had already told me that Marcus had an elaborate security system. He knew that Sawn-Off was an occasional visitor and had probably just seen him on camera prior to his obvious Punch and bowl clue.

TRENCH: Brilliant, old timer.

OLD TOM: And the maid, Gemma had to be the missing Emmy. Why call your servant by their Christian name? The aristocracy simply doesn't do that. It struck me as over-familiarity. The dropped milk, when you first mentioned Emma, Trench. Marcus and his maid were often seen together - and you even saw them kiss, eventually. Also their closeness was the likely reason that Marcus spurned Sally-Anne's advances in the dead of night...

TRENCH: Yes, I can see the clues building up, creating a near-complete picture.

OLD TOM: And inevitably there's the clincher.

TRENCH: You've lost me, old boy.

OLD TOM: Marcus really was toying with you. He said there was no gee gees at Dreadbury.

TRENCH: Yes, because of Emmy's apparent allergy to horses.

OLD TOM: No gee gees – odd language, if I may say so. No Gs. Take the G away from Gemma…

TRENCH: And you get Emma, another name for Emmy – of course.

OLD TOM: And if you add the clues to Marcus' and Emmy's motivation for being rid of Sawn-Off and the Syndicate, the picture is not only complete, but also framed.

TRENCH: And framed beautifully, may I say? Although we can't really use this as a story for the Stokeham Herald. Sally-Anne's forthcoming expose on the Landlord's shenanigans at the Cock and Pheasant will help a bit, though.

OLD TOM: I'm glad.

TRENCH: So, the manor-house mystery has been solved by the Armchair Detective.

OLD TOM: You played your part well too, Trench. Away in the field, so to speak.

TRENCH: Praise indeed.

OLD TOM: Well, Trench do pop in again if you stumble across another case in desperate need of 'solvation'.

TRENCH: I will. Goodbye then, Old Tom.

OLD TOM: Before you do go though, Trench - go and
make the tea again. You did such a good job last time. You know,
through the hallway, turn...

TRENCH: Yes, I remember where the kitchen is.

                           *(We hear TRENCH get up and walk to the
kitchen. He turns the kettle on.)*

TRENCH: *(Who shouts from the kitchen.)* Hang on, like
last time, we'll have to wait for the tea to cool down. Which means I'll
be here for ages.

OLD TOM: *(Who chuckles.)* Yes, young Trench, I suppose
you will.

        CLOSING MYSTERY MUSIC

THE

ARMCHAIR

DETECTIVE

and the

CELEBRITY

STALKER

INTRODUCTION

"My name is Darnia Storm. I was a stunning glamour model, now I'm a beautiful actress. I adore men - and love women. But not everyone shares my amazing success. Jealousy and bitterness are now my co-stars. Someone is stalking me, but who? I need help..."

Trench takes the Lead, and Old Tom directs the Show from backstage...

The Celebrity Stalker *is a traditional whodunit. And perhaps suffers slightly because of the linear plot. However, hopefully the twist at the end makes up for this as well as the creation of the seductive legend that is Darnia Storm.*

CAST LIST

TRENCH

OLD TOM

SALLY-ANNE

EDITOR LAW

DARNIA STORM

DONNY DAVIES

VIVIEN VELVET

BEN

DIRECTOR

ACT ONE

OPENING MYSTERY MUSIC

(There is a knock on the front door.)

OLD TOM: Do come in, young man, the door is open.

(We hear TRENCH enter the flat and settle down opposite OLD TOM.)

TRENCH: You've just made yourself a cup of tea, Old Tom – it's steaming.

OLD TOM: Yes, it will be quite a while before it's cold enough to drink.

TRENCH: And it's been quite a while since all that business at the Manor-House.

OLD TOM: That was a particularly absorbing mystery and there is nothing, young Trench that I find more absorbing than an absorbing mystery. So, what particular story at the Stokeham Herald can I unleash my investigative mind on today?

TRENCH: Err, that stunning glamour model-turned-actress, Darnia Storm is appearing in a Play all next week at the Stokeham Empire.

OLD TOM: *(Sounds bored all of a sudden.)* And how can I help you with that?

TRENCH: Does there always have to be some sort of case to solve? Can't I come here just to simply see you? Is that a crime?

OLD TOM: My time here, Trench is very valuable. I will not waste a minute of it on idle chatter or on a so-called celebrity who can't even act.

TRENCH: I'm sorry to have troubled you then. I don't think I'll bother coming here again.

OLD TOM: It is probably best you don't. I am not here just to talk, only to help.

TRENCH: Well, Old Tom, from now on I'll try to report my stories without your help.

OLD TOM: Good for you, Trenchy.

TRENCH: I'll be off then.

OLD TOM: Goodbye.

TRENCH: And I'll never come back, unless I become really stuck, of course.

OLD TOM: *(Who chuckles softly.)* Of course.

                (We hear TRENCH leave the old man.)

                (Music moves on the time and scene.)

(We hear TRENCH shuffling his papers about on his desk and tut-tutting.)

SALLY-ANNE   What is wrong with you, Trench?

TRENCH: Nothing, why should anything be wrong?

SALLY-ANNE   You've been making a nuisance of yourself all afternoon. You've been quite remote, awkward, ignorant, grumbling to yourself and generally making the office look untidy. Come to think of it, Trenchy – you are actually just being your usual self.

TRENCH: *(Says slowly with a heavy hint of sarcasm:)* Hah, hah – very funny, Sally-Anne.

SALLY-ANNE: You nearly managed something half-resembling a smile then. Congratulations

TRENCH: If you must know, me and Old Tom are finished.

SALLY-ANNE: I didn't know you were going out together!

TRENCH: Will you let me know when you've taken your funny head off, and then we can have a proper conversation?

SALLY-ANNE: Sorry, I know how fond you are of your cosy little chats with Old Thomas. What's happened, had a lover's tiff or something? Oops, at it again.

TRENCH: Right that's it, Sally-Anne – I'm not telling you now.

SALLY-ANNE: Oh come on, Trench. Really, have you had a disagreement?

TRENCH: He virtually threw me out of his damned Mayflower flat. He complained that I wasn't there to discuss a new story or case. Obviously it's a problem to have an innocent chat with an old friend.

SALLY-ANNE: Tom may be old, Trench – but isn't he really more of a new friend?

TRENCH: Oh, you know what I mean.

SALLY-ANNE: Do you want me to go and have a talk with him?

TRENCH: No. Old Tom doesn't seem to like strangers or visitors of any kind in fact.

SALLY-ANNE: Including you at the moment.

TRENCH: Except when I have some sort of baffling mystery to solve, then Old Tom's all ears.

SALLY-ANNE: So it's simple then – we just need a story with an intriguing puzzle to bring you two love-birds back together. I must stop that.

          (The door creaks open further and busy footsteps are heard.)

TRENCH: Ah, Editor Law – what can we do for you?

EDITOR LAW: Playing nicely children? Yes..? Well in that case, may I introduce you to, Miss Darnia Storm.

          (We hear intakes of breath as the sound of DARNIA's stilettoes are heard entering the office.)

SALLY-ANNE: Close your mouth, Trench. Electric fly-traps are all that's necessary for this building.

TRENCH: Stunning, truly beautiful...

DARNIA: I beg your pardon.

TRENCH: I mean Storm, Miss Storm – truly a beautiful name.

DARNIA: Oh call me Darnia please, darling – all my friends do.

EDITOR LAW: This is Trench and his colleague Sally-Anne.

SALLY-ANNE: Excuse me Editor Law, but I won't have that. Trench is my colleague, not... Ooh, how nice – who is that gorgeous, err gentleman behind you, dear?

DARNIA: Oh, that's just Ben Brown. He's my bodyguard.

EDITOR LAW: Right, now that all the introductions are over with, I think it's time we got down to business.

DARNIA: Yes, I assume this is the show business department of the Paper?

SALLY-ANNE: I'm afraid not, Darnia. The Stokeham Herald doesn't exactly stretch to having a show...

EDITOR LAW: ... a showstopper section – that's what we call it. Although unlike your profession Miss Storm, there are no stars here.

TRENCH: Speak for yourself, boss.

(DARNIA laughs.)

EDITOR LAW: But we all like to muck in anyway. And yes, this is the section of my esteemed newspaper that handles all the showbiz gossip; I mean show business related items.

DARNIA: I'm satisfied, so I'll 'cut to the chase' – as I said in a B movie that I'm not terribly proud of.

(TRENCH sniggers.)

DARNIA: I have come here for your help. I am being... stalked – and I want you to expose the psycho that's bothering me.

SALLY-ANNE: Shouldn't you be going to the police about this, or at least a private detective?

DARNIA: Dear girl, the police would basically mean going public and my experience with private-eyes in the past has proved them unreliable.

SALLY-ANNE: Journalists aren't exactly known for their discretion, you know.

DARNIA: Which brings me to the deal. In return for keeping quiet and discovering the identity of my sick stalker, you have my promise of an exclusive on this story – and my amazing life so far. Well, what do you say?

EDITOR LAW: They agree to your deal, Miss Storm – unreservedly. This could be the making of this Paper.

DARNIA: What is your reaction, Trench?

TRENCH: I'll have to stalk, I mean follow you around. I'll need to stalk, sorry talk to you further; watch you when you are performing – in fact become part of your life to achieve what you are asking for.

DARNIA: I will look forward to it. I am appearing all next week in 'Model Murder' at your Stokeham Empire theatre. And what about you, Sally-Anne?

SALLY-ANNE: Oh, I'll need your bodyguard, Ben's number – purely for the sake of the investigation of course.

BEN: I will be protecting my mistress – and I am the best bodyguard outside Chicago, so I am not easily distracted.

SALLY-ANNE: Err, if you say so.

DARNIA: So, my dear Sally-Anne – if you want Ben, you'll have to go through me first.

SALLY-ANNE: *(Who clears her throat.)* I'll bear that in mind.

DARNIA: Your Editor Law here has the details of where you can find me. Goodbye my two friends – for now.

EDITOR LAW: I'll see you out.

(We hear them leave.)

TRENCH: Well, what do you make of that, Sally-Anne?

SALLY-ANNE: I think she was coming on to both of us!

TRENCH: Yes, I have a feeling that this case will be very, very interesting. And do you know what's going to be even better?

SALLY-ANNE: What?

TRENCH: It looks like I'm going to have an excuse to visit Old Tom again after all.

SALLY-ANNE: *(Says in a withering tone:)* Oh, Trench.

(Music with a comedic touch, followed by a tune with an air of seduction changes scene.)

(There is a careful knock on the door.)

DARNIA: Who's there?

TRENCH: It's me Trench, Darnia. The hotel receptionist should have said I was coming up.

DARNIA: I know, with everything that is happening at the moment, I was just making sure.

(We hear DARNIA remove a couple of chains; withdraw a bolt; unlock the door and eventually open it.)

DARNIA: Drink Trench? Like me, my mini-bar is very accommodating.

TRENCH: Why don't you surprise me, dear Darnia?

DARNIA: I like surprising people. You're looking very smart, by the way.

TRENCH: But not as, dare I say it, as sensationally sexy as you. That revealing skirt certainly shows off your shapely legs to their full potential. Wait a second, can you stop me? Or I'll need a cold shower.

(We hear DARNIA finish with the mini-bar.)

DARNIA: Will a champagne spritzer calm you down?

TRENCH: I'm not sure, but I'm prepared to give it a try.

DARNIA: Cheers.

(They clink their glasses together and start drinking.)

TRENCH: Mm excellent Darnia. Bubbly but sharp.

DARNIA: A bit like me, then. Where's the lovely Sally-Anne?

TRENCH: Indisposed, I'm afraid.

DARNIA: Shame. I was looking forward to meeting her in my hotel bedroom...

TRENCH: *(His voice slightly high.)* Do you realise that your hand is rubbing my thigh?

DARNIA: Of course I do, Trench. But my hand is only moving gently, ever so gently...

TRENCH: Before we get carried away, I thought you wanted to talk about your so-called stalker.

(The caressing suddenly stops.)

DARNIA: You know how to bring a girl down to earth, I'll give you that.

TRENCH: Sorry.

DARNIA: We might as well sit down in the adjoining suite.

(They move to the next room and sit down on a sumptuous sofa.)

TRENCH: Now this is a sofa you could sink in.

DARNIA: Quite. Well, unfortunately there is nothing so-called about the thing that stalks me. He is as real as you or I.

TRENCH: You know he is a he then?

DARNIA: Most of my fans are male. They are more than aware of my glamorous model days. Although I do have a strong female following too.

TRENCH: So, the stalker could be male or female. I'm glad we've sorted that out!

DARNIA: Don't make fun of me. I'm liable to pounce on anybody that makes fun of me.

TRENCH: According to the tabloid newspapers, you're liable to pounce on anybody full stop – causing a storm wherever you go.

DARNIA: Yes darling, they seem to like playing around with my surname.

TRENCH: Right. Family and friends, where are they Darnia?

DARNIA: My parents and real friends are still in my native Sweden.

TRENCH: We can virtually cross them off our suspect list then. Silly question but, any lovers?

DARNIA: Yes, and frequently. But I'm not going to mention them, besides there is nobody serious because I'm serious about love, but not seriously in love.

TRENCH: All right, I can always check the tabloids for this weeks' rumours and gossip. So let's list the people closer to home to you right now.

DARNIA: Well there's my manager, Donny Davies who is also staying at this hotel, helping me to promote my Play. Oh, and I suppose the entire cast of 'Model Murder'.

TRENCH: And your bodyguard Ben – where is he, by the way?

DARNIA: Ben? Oh yes, Sally-Anne liked him. He is only employed to protect me outside of the hotel – and of the theatre.

TRENCH: And the stalker himself. What has he – or she – actually done to you so far?

DARNIA: Come Trench, I'll show you...

(Thoughtful music changes scene and time.)

SALLY-ANNE: Well, that's the dodgy double-glazing story wrapped. Trenchy, and how did you fare with the flirtatious Miss Storm?

TRENCH: Investigations are continuing...

SALLY-ANNE: I'll be blunt then – did she seduce you or not? This time you've been more careful about the lipstick marks. I can't find a trace...

TRENCH: Sally-Anne, don't examine me too closely – I may kiss you instead.

SALLY-ANNE: In that case, I'll sit behind my desk like a good girl.

(We hear her do just that.)

SALLY-ANNE: Well?

TRENCH: I'm going to confine my revelations to the story.

SALLY-ANNE: That means you probably didn't get together then.

TRENCH: She wanted to though.

SALLY-ANNE: Big head.

TRENCH: Darnia is irresistible and yet I resisted her. Now, why did I do that?

SALLY-ANNE: You decided to exercise that virtually extinct quality in our profession: journalistic integrity.

TRENCH: Something like that. Sexy Miss Storm did enquire after you though, Sally. She was most upset that you weren't there with me…

SALLY-ANNE: Don't start that again, Trench. She's behaving more and more like her football wife character from that dreadful television series, 'Sporting Spouses'.

TRENCH: Yes, glam model turned actress. She also featured in a few dodgy horror films which generally involve her screaming in skimpy outfits, that I err happened to watch – a bit.

SALLY-ANNE: And onto that TV series before landing a role in a theatrical tour which starts here.

TRENCH: I wonder why it didn't begin in the West End? Most Plays do.

SALLY-ANNE: They probably demanded a bit of actual acting – and that's something dear Darnia Storm isn't very good at.

TRENCH: After the threats I saw, her next part may be, 'The Victim'.

SALLY-ANNE: But who's playing the title-role of, 'The Stalker'..?

(*Thoughtful music with a kind of sensationalism ends the scene.*)

OLD TOM: Come in, young man – the door is open.

TRENCH: I might have known.

(*We hear TRENCH enter the flat and OLD TOM's living room.*)

TRENCH: It's all right, Old Tom – there's no need to get up from that beloved armchair of yours.

OLD TOM: You know me better than that.

TRENCH: So, are we still friends?

OLD TOM: Our relationship has not changed, if that's what you mean. All you require to realise is that our time together is very precious – so don't waste it.

TRENCH: Agreed.

OLD TOM: Right, as you can see young Trench, I have some stale cake left over and there is more cold tea in the pot, so would you like..?

TRENCH: 'A cup of tea an' slice o 'cake'? Yes, yes I would. Wait a minute, why are you being so nice to me? How do you know I'm not here for another meaningless chat and therefore wasting your time?

OLD TOM: I have greater respect for your intelligence than that, Trench. While you're pouring the tea, tell me what's on your mind...

(*A brief interlude of music passes some time.*)

OLD TOM: So, how fascinating - and challenging: to discover the mystery stalker of stage star, Darnia Storm.

TRENCH: Challenging?

OLD TOM: Well yes, in theory the anonymous antagonist could be virtually anyone in the country – but first let's concentrate on the people close to Miss Storm.

TRENCH: All we have so far then is: her dedicated bodyguard, Ben Brown; her manager – a Donny Davies whom I haven't met yet who is, incidentally, staying in the same hotel; the cast of 'Model Murder'; an ex-lover – I've heard there's plenty of them, or a fan who's perhaps become too fanatic?

OLD TOM: Or an elaborate publicity stunt by madam Darnia herself. The 'keep the stalker secret' promise she made you keep could be a clever double-bluff.

TRENCH: So, is this all a 'storm in a teacup' or is it something more serious?

OLD TOM: Those threatening letters – all from newspaper cuttings.

                (We hear OLD TOM click his fingers.)

TRENCH: Yes, here – have another look.

                (We hear OLD TOM study the letters.)

OLD TOM: 'I'm watching you'. 'I can smell you'. 'Your next performance will be your last'. 'You must seek greater protection'. 'I am your death'.

TRENCH: Yes, it sounds serious and rather disturbing. So, Old Tom, what do you think?

OLD TOM: I think a storm is brewing…

                (Mystery music indicates the end of Act One.)

ACT TWO

SALLY-ANNE: Well Trench, have you two kissed and made up?

TRENCH: You mean me and Old Tom, yes. Hey, what do you mean 'kissed and... Sally-Anne, you're teasing me again.

SALLY-ANNE: All right then, did the old mucker shed any light on this stalker story then?

TRENCH: Not really. Our investigations are only at a preliminary stage and as my elderly friend pointed out, the suspect could be anyone – even you!

SALLY-ANNE: Oh behave. OK, whilst you two were no doubt drinking tea and eating hob-knobs or whatever it is you do; it's a good job someone was actually doing something useful.

TRENCH: And I suppose that someone is you?

SALLY-ANNE: Oh, hi Editor Law. Yes, we are still busy on the stalker Storm and no – we don't know who it is yet.

EDITOR LAW: Sally-Anne, do you usually answer someone else's questions before they've even asked them? I would say it's the height of bad manners.

SALLY-ANNE: Sor-ry.

TRENCH: And no, Editor – I've nothing to add. Oops, I've done it too.

EDITOR LAW: Typical, absolutely typical.

(We hear EDITOR LAW walk away from the office.)

SALLY-ANNE: Now, where was I?

TRENCH: You were just about to tell me how awfully clever you've been, while I was having a natter with Old Tom.

SALLY-ANNE: (Who giggles slightly before speaking.) Oh yes, I delved into the production company and cast of 'Model Murder' and it seems one particular actress has one hell of a motive for unsettling Darnia Storm.

TRENCH: I'm listening.

SALLY-ANNE: Vivien Velvet has just completed a successful tour in the West End and it was her who originally was offered the role of the heroine in the new Play. But when Darnia became available, Vivien was immediately demoted to a supporting role.

TRENCH: Interesting, even the most sympathetic of actresses might feel a twinge of envy and resentment in such circumstances.

SALLY-ANNE: And let's face it, we all know what bitches prima-divas can be...

TRENCH: The question is, are the claws drawn..?

SALLY-ANNE: ...and ready to tear into Miss Storm?

(Ominous music changes the scene.)

(TRENCH and SALLY-ANNE are walking along the streets of Stokeham.)

SALLY-ANNE: So, how come this Vivien Velvet is not staying at the hotel?

TRENCH: She's staying with a friend of the family, I believe. Probably a lot cheaper...

SALLY-ANNE: Or friendlier...

TRENCH: Ah, here we are Sall. Remember we are not to reveal anything about the stalker, so be careful what you say.

SALLY-ANNE: And remember you are not talking to that brain-box, Happy now – and remember that it was my enquiries that has actually led us here, Trenchy.

TRENCH: Point taken.

(TRENCH knocks on the front door. After a few moments, we here it open.)

SALLY-ANNE: Miss Vivien Velvet, I believe. I'm Sally-Anne and this is Trench – we are journalists for the Stokeham Herald, hoping to publicise your forthcoming Play. May we have a quick interview?

VIVIEN: Identification?

TRENCH: Of course.

(We hear then take out their Press Passes and show them to VIVIEN.)

VIVIEN: They seem satisfactory – can't be too careful these days. By rights, you first should be talking to the production company's Press Officer, but I don't think that a little chat will do any harm. Come in.

SALLY-ANNE: Thank-you.

(They enter the house.)

VIVIEN: Please, sit down. Now, what would you like to ask me?

TRENCH: How would you describe the Play, Miss Velvet?

VIVIEN: 'Model Murder' is a whodunit, thriller with a twist. There are moments of humour and real suspense; a sense of danger...

SALLY-ANNE: Forgive me, but I have read your glowing reviews from the West End.

VIVIEN: I appreciate you noticing... Sally.

SALLY-ANNE: What I can't understand is why you're not playing the lead – the heroine?

VIVIEN: I was... until *(says sarcastically:)* delightful Darnia came along. She puts bums on seats, the director so crudely said – and ironically, Darnia herself has biggest one of all.

TRENCH: *(Who, unsuccessfully, tries to supress a laugh.)* So, how did Darnia Storm land the role, then?

VIVIEN: Apart from being notoriously famous? Basically she has slept with the director, the producer and the lead actor. She even tried it on with me! – to try to get me on her side. That talentless trollop will have what's coming to her one day.

SALLY-ANNE: And what's that, Miss Velvet?

VIVIEN: Trouble. Miss Storm attracts trouble, and soon she'll have much more than even she can handle.

TRENCH: And then you can take over?

VIVIEN: You catch on quick, boy. Anyway, don't you think that velvet is superior to tarty rags?

(More music moves time on.)

(TRENCH and SALLY-ANNE are once again outside, walking along the pavement.)

SALLY-ANNE: So, if Vivien Velvet hasn't got a motive for bothering Darnia Storm, I'm Happy's smarter sister.

TRENCH: That explains a lot!

SALLY-ANNE: Hey!

TRENCH: Yes, Vivien the vixen may have a motive – but that doesn't necessarily mean she is our man, err so to speak.

SALLY-ANNE: Well, she's definitely top of my suspect list. What about you, Trench?

TRENCH: The problem is that there isn't really many suspects to list, so it's time to find out more. I think I'll pay Darnia's manager – Mr Davies a visit.

SALLY-ANNE: You do that Trenchy. I'll go back to the office and start playing catch-up. 'The Paper…

TRENCH: …won't write itself' – I know.

SALLY-ANNE: Don't miss me too much then.

(We hear SALLY-ANNE start to walk away.)

TRENCH: *(Who raises his voice.)* Sally-Anne – wait.

(*SALLY-ANNE sighs, obviously reluctantly stopping.*)

SALLY-ANNE: Well, what is it?

TRENCH: When you're done – can you come and meet me at the hotel?

SALLY-ANNE: I suppose so – why?

TRENCH: It will be time to have another chat with our supposed 'victim', Miss Storm.

SALLY-ANNE: I'm not sure whether I like where this is leading…

TRENCH: If you could have an intimate chat with Darnia alone, you may get more out of her.

SALLY-ANNE: That's what worries me.

TRENCH: Come on, I'm sure she is keeping vital information from us. She will have her reasons, but what are they?

SALLY-ANNE: All right then – I'll do it. But I want you nearby – for protection.

TRENCH: Don't worry Sally, I'll heroically defend your honour, if need be.

SALLY-ANNE: (*Says in a doubting, high-pitched voice:*) Wonderful.

(*A brief spell of mystery music moves things along.*)

TRENCH: Mr Davies, I presume – I'm the journalist you…

DONNY: Ah, Trench – yes, yes you called earlier. Come in and call me Donny, all my enemies do.

(*TRENCH enters the hotel room and sits down.*)

DONNY: Drink?

TRENCH: Oh not this early in the day – thanks. Enemies you were saying?

DONNY: Just my little joke, that's all. Right, down to business, I want you to devote most of your local rag – I mean newspaper to the delights of Darnia Storm and her model Play – ha, slight play on words there. In fact, I want your front page headlines to be 'Darnia's Model Murder Goes Down A Storm'. With any luck, a couple of the nationals will pick up on it and then...

TRENCH: Woe, woe, woe. Hang on Mr Davies, err Donny. I am not the editor of the Stokeham Herald. Although I'll be writing a feature on your actress stroke model, I couldn't possibly hand the Paper over to you.

DONNY: OK, but we need something and something big. The theatre bookings are only half-full. For Darnia's career – and the Play – to really take off, we need to generate a massive publicity stunt, something like a... like a...

TRENCH: ...a secret stalker threatening her from the shadows?

DONNY: Brilliant!

TRENCH: Yes Donny, but mighten that encourage unwanted attention from certain undesirables.

DONNY: There's always that danger and anyway, I'll look after her. But, yes – a stalker. We'll hit every tabloid, never mind one. There's even a surreal connection to the Play: 'Model Murder' – get it? And I want you to start those stalker rumours flying, Trench.

TRENCH: (Says quietly:) Those rumours would actually be real ones.

DONNY: What was that, Trench?

TRENCH: I'll suggest the rumours in my features discreetly, to make them sound more realistic.

DONNY: Well don't be too discreet. The public round 'ere aren't noted for reading in-between the lines – do me a favour and make it, at least, a bit obvious... and then the Storm Stalker storyline can grip the nation!

TRENCH: *(Says under his breath:)* What have I done?

(A brief interlude of music passes a little time.)

TRENCH: Yes, I will – goodbye Mr Donny Davies.

(We hear TRENCH close the door with some relief.)

TRENCH: Impossible, the man's impossible.

SALLY-ANNE: Are you talking about Darnia's manager or your Old Tom again?

TRENCH: Very funny. Sally-Anne you do look err, attractive. Knee-length black skirt; dark silk stockings – a revealing blouse, Darnia is going to be very pleased to see you.

SALLY-ANNE: They are not silk stockings, Trenchy. Don't allow your sordid fantasies to completely carry you away.

TRENCH: I'd better have a cold shower, then.

SALLY-ANNE: You do that. I am dressed up though because I thought the point of the exercise is to tempt Darnia to reveal more than she perhaps wants to.

TRENCH: Ahem – and exactly.

SALLY-ANNE: And I am talking about information relating to this alleged stranger who's been supposedly bothering her.

TRENCH: Well, what are you waiting for Sall? Darnia's suite is just there.

SALLY-ANNE: Where will you be, Trench? I want you in the room, with me – just in case.

TRENCH: Come on, how can I? Wait, when you go in – distract her – and I'll slip into the bathroom.

SALLY-ANNE: Yes – ideal. You can have your cold shower, after all.

(Hectic music moves a bit of time along.)

TRENCH: *(Who whispers:)* Right, I'm in the bathroom – now forget about me.

SALLY-ANNE: Right.

DARNIA: Here's your champagne Sally – who were you speaking to?

SALLY-ANNE: I was just saying I'm right looking forward to this champagne, it's not often a girl like me has the chance…

DARNIA: I always have the chance – and I take it. Come, sit down next to me.

(DARNIA pats and strokes the sofa.)

SALLY-ANNE: All right.

(SALLY-ANNE sits down slowly.)

DARNIA: May I say how beautiful you're looking, Sally. You have a gorgeous figure.

SALLY-ANNE: I'm not surprised with all that running around I do, after Trench. You have a pretty special figure yourself, Darnia – you have a bust to die for and that slit in your dress is very revealing.

DARNIA: Ah, you've noticed – have a closer look at my shapely legs, Sally.

(We hear DARNIA place her thigh across SALLY.)

DARNIA: You can touch it, if you want.

SALLY-ANNE: (Who whispers:) I think I need that cold shower!

DARNIA: What was that sexy? Come closer, I want you.

SALLY-ANNE: And I... Oops, I'm sorry.

DARNIA: (Says slightly frustrated:) You've spilt your champagne all over me. I must go to the bathroom.

SALLY-ANNE: Err – no!

DARNIA: (Then continues with casual seductiveness:) You mean I can always take my wet dress off in the bedroom?

TRENCH: I wonder if they'll hear me, if I really do take that cold shower?

SALLY-ANNE: Before things move out of control, Darnia – let's talk about this stalker business more, and then perhaps we can continue...

(Seductive music passes some more time.)

DARNIA: Right, that's enough about me – even though myself is my favourite subject. Let me now show you the bedroom, Sally.

SALLY-ANNE: I would truly love to see it, but I really must be going. (Then says loudly:) Trench will be waiting for me.

DARNIA: Perhaps some other time...

(There is a loud knock on the door.)

DARNIA: (Who snaps:) What is it?

(The door opens.)

DARNIA: Ben, what do you want? I don't need protection in here.

SALLY-ANNE: *(Says quietly:)* No, but I do.

BEN: As instructed, I was keeping an eye on the comings and goings of the hotel.

DARNIA: Who..? Never mind. What are you carrying?

BEN: It's an urgent parcel for Darnia Storm which is you, of course. I took it from the courier.

DARNIA: Let's open it then.

TRENCH: No, it might be something dangerous.

DARNIA: Trench, how did you..?

TRENCH: Err, the door's open.

DONNY: What's all this commotion going on?

DARNIA: Donny – does anybody else want to come into my room, while we're at it?

BEN: I'm the bodyguard, I'll open the package.

DARNIA: Be my guest.

SALLY-ANNE: Is it ticking, Trench?

TRENCH: Sally-Anne, please take your fingers out of your ears...

(Music with more than a bit of danger changes scene and time.)

OLD TOM: Hmm, that last drop of cold tea really hits the spot. Young Trench, I'd be obliged if you would be good enough to check out the biscuit situation.

TRENCH: Certainly, Old Tom.

(We hear TRENCH open the metal lid.)

TRENCH: Poo, these biscuits smell.

OLD TOM: I know, very tempting.

TRENCH: If you say so.

OLD TOM: I'll take one for now and save one for later. Now, where were we?

TRENCH: I was just touching upon Darnia's conversation with Sally-Anne about the star's past.

OLD TOM: (Who just finishes munching a biscuit.) Well, go on Trench – I don't have all day.

TRENCH: (Who sighs.) Sally steered Darnia – I think reluctantly to talk about a former lover, someone from long ago who was courting her as she left school. When pressed, all Darnia would say about him was that she doesn't see him anymore but he's still around.

OLD TOM: How very interesting...

TRENCH: Which points to our suspect being a man...

OLD TOM: That accepts the assumption that Ms Storm's ex and the stalker are one and the same – which may not be necessarily so. And the 'bomb' incident you mentioned earlier – run that by me again – it just doesn't seem to ring true.

TRENCH: As I've said – Ben the bodyguard brought the package into the room 'interrupting' Darnia and Sally. I 'entered' and so did her manager, Donny Davies. Ben opened the parcel and then…

OLD TOM: … bang!

TRENCH: Bang, literally. A flag popped up with 'bang!' on, and a message underneath.

OLD TOM: Yes, 'You're next performance will be a dead one'. Which implies a theatrical connection.

TRENCH: Vivien Velvet?

OLD TOM: She certainly seems to have more reason than most – in a prima-donna-diva sort of way. It may be a good idea to keep an eye on rehearsals though, Trench.

TRENCH: You think the danger is connected to the Play?

OLD TOM: Possibly, but not let's disregard our other stalker suspects. It was Ben who brought the package to Ms Storm. Does that imply he is involved or merely stupid? You don't open mysterious packages at a time of possible danger, right in front of the person you're trying to protect!

TRENCH: No you don't. But, whilst Ben isn't quite as bad as Happy, I don't think he's the sharpest pencil in the case.

OLD TOM: And her manager, Donny Davies. He even thought the stalker idea was good for publicity!

TRENCH: Now, we're overflowing with suspects and I'm still suspicious of Darnia herself! So, Old Tom – what next?

OLD TOM: I would like photographs of Ms Storm's earlier modelling career – especially pictures showing her left hand.

TRENCH: Are you sure you're not just being a dirty old man?

OLD TOM: I wasn't the one who re-told me of young Sally's encounter with Ms Storm with, shall we say, such enthusiasm.

TRENCH: You have me there, Old Tom.

OLD TOM: About those pictures I requested?

TRENCH: Oh yes, I could retrieve the photos from Newspaper Archives, but what a strange request: left hand indeed?

OLD TOM: We are slowly approaching the last act, Trench.

TRENCH: I know, I just don't want it to be the final curtain for Darnia Storm…

(Mystery music indicates the end of Act Two.)

ACT THREE

SALLY-ANNE: To put it mildly, I've had an eventful day and have completed this huge pile of work here.

(SALLY-ANNE slaps the pile of papers.)

SALLY-ANNE: Editor Law has gone home, so I think I will join him.

TRENCH: Really, Sally-Anne – you're going home with Editor Law? I didn't realise you were so close!

SALLY-ANNE: Hah... hah... hah. You know very well what I meant, Trenchy. I need a long soak in a hot, soapy bath.

TRENCH: Except that you don't have time for a bath. Old Tom thinks we should keep an eye on rehearsals. Darnia is due at the theatre shortly, so we'd better be going.

SALLY-ANNE: I'm sorry – I didn't realise I was now working for good Old Tom. Silly me – I was under the misapprehension that Editor Law was somehow our boss!

TRENCH: Silly girl – you should know better. You know Old Tom's advice makes sense though.

SALLY-ANNE: Trench, I'm knack... err very tired – can't you go on your own?

TRENCH: Come on Sall – I need you there. If our enigmatic stalker does turn up, an extra pair of eyes could be very useful. Please Sally-Anne. And besides, I hate going to the theatre alone.

SALLY-ANNE: *(Says resignedly with a sigh:)* Oh, go on then.

TRENCH: You might also have a chance to reacquaint yourself with the beautiful Miss Storm.

SALLY-ANNE: Tell you what, why don't I stalk you and then start strangling...

(We hear the rustling of newspaper.)

TRENCH: Actually after checking this paper, Darnia won't be treading the boards yet, anyway. Rehearsals don't begin till tomorrow morning. So, enjoy your bath!

(Quirky music changes the scene.)

SALLY-ANNE: Where shall we sit?

VIVIEN: Do you mind – believe it or not we are trying to rehearse in here.

SALLY-ANNE: Sorry Vivien – carry on. *(Then says more quietly:)* Trench, where shall we sit?

TRENCH: Well, as the theatre is completely empty, we are somewhat spoilt for choice. So, how about the front row?

SALLY-ANNE: Right. *(Then says more quietly:)* Right.

(We hear TRENCH and SALLY-ANNE shuffle to the front row and finally sit down.)

TRENCH: It's just Darnia and Vivien Velvet on stage at the moment.

SALLY-ANNE: So, let's listen then – shall we?

TRENCH: Excuse me Sally-Anne. I wasn't the one who was told off for talking loudly.

SALLY-ANNE: Shh.

DARNIA: *(Who's acting on stage.)* Three of my models have been murdered and you, detective, are telling me to carry on as though nothing has happened.

VIVIEN: *(As the detective.)* Our man is closing in – and one more model shoot, if you will excuse the expression, is all I should need to apprehend our assailant. *(Then says in her own voice:)* Oh come on, director.

DIRECTOR: *(The voice comes from near the back of the theatre.)* What is it now, Vivien? Why can't you be a good girl like Darnia?

VIVIEN: *(Says furiously:)* I'm sorry, but Darnia is neither good nor bad – she is awful. She is putting the wrong emotional emphasis on virtually all her lines. She is a complete amateur – and that is 'what's the matter'.

DARNIA: Oh Vivien darling, drop the vixen act. It's becoming so predictable – and boring.

VIVIEN: Are you going to let her speak to me like that? I mean, she has all the best lines – and she's killing every one of them.

DIRECTOR: Come on ladies, stop squabbling. Just say the lines, and let me worry about the 'emotional emphases'.

(DARNIA laughs in a superior way.)

VIVIEN: Right that's it. I must have talent to work with. Goodbye – and good riddance. If you beg me, I may return as the star – when you've sacked that!

(VIVIEN loudly storms off through the seating area.)

SALLY-ANNE: What a drama queen.

TRENCH: That's exactly what Vivien is. Mind you, Darnia does seem to create a storm wherever she goes...

DIRECTOR: Darnia, you might as well take a break.

DARNIA: In a minute. I'm just going to practice my stage positioning for a few moments.

SALLY-ANNE: It looks like that's the end of the show.

(Suddenly there is an almighty crash and a terrible scream.)

TRENCH: Darnia! Are you all right?

DIRECTOR: Somebody call an ambulance.

SALLY-ANNE: What happened?

TRENCH: A sandbag fell from high above the stage. Come, we'd better see if Darnia is hurt.

(We hear TRENCH and SALLY-ANNE frantically climb the stage.)

TRENCH: Darnia..?

SALLY-ANNE: It's Sally-Anne, Darnia.

DARNIA: Oh my head – I must have banged it when I fell. Luckily though, the sandbag just missed me.

SALLY-ANNE: It could have been a terrible accident...

TRENCH: If it was an accident.

DARNIA: You mean... my stalker? I could have died. Yes, his last warning was that 'my next part will be a dead one'.

TRENCH: And this time Darnia, your mystery stalker was almost right.

(Music reflecting impending danger changes scene.)

(TRENCH and SALLY-ANNE are clearly outside the theatre as we hear associated traffic noises etc.)

SALLY-ANNE: Well, Trench – did your backstage investigation reveal anything?

TRENCH: Only that the 'accident' was no accident. I had to climb quite high above the stage, on the gantry, and the rope that connects the curtains to the counter-weight of the sandbag...

SALLY-ANNE: Get on with it.

TRENCH: As I was saying before I was rudely interrupted, the rope had been cut clean through. We nearly witnessed a very deliberate attempt at murder.

SALLY-ANNE: So the stalker has become much more than simply threatening – but why? As background to this story, I've studied psychological profiles of the typical stalker and in nearly all cases they huff and puff and threaten all sorts of dreadful things but they always fall short of actual direct action.

TRENCH: So, what makes this case different?

SALLY-ANNE: If we can discover that, we will have our man – or woman. Is Darnia going to be all right?

TRENCH: I think so – all Miss Storm would say when I went back to her was that from now on she would have Ben with her to protect her all the time. Basically she now won't let her bodyguard out of her sight.

SALLY-ANNE: Which probably takes care of her immediate safety.

TRENCH: Yes, Sally-Anne, probably...

SALLY-ANNE: Well Trench, I know Editor Law has given us plenty of time on this Story, but now we have the afternoon free, hadn't we better catch up on some of our less glamorous stories and actually do some work?

TRENCH: *(Says unenthusiastically:)* You mean write about parking problems and dogs messing the pavements? Come on, let's go back to the office.

(Music with irony ends the scene.)

TRENCH: I didn't know you could be fined one thousand pounds if your dog has an unfortunate accident on the pavement. Did you know you could be fined one thousand pounds if your...

SALLY-ANNE: All right Trench, I get the message. And yes, I did know. Right that just about wraps our work up today and whatever you say, I am going home. What about you?

TRENCH: First I'm going to nip to Newspaper Archives to retrieve some pictures Old Tom requested and then, I think I'll pay our favourite hotel another visit.

SALLY-ANNE: Do you want to carry on where I left off with Darnia?

TRENCH: Not quite, Sally-Anne. I am more interested in having another chat with that manager of hers – Donny Davies.

SALLY-ANNE: Do you think he's hiding something?

TRENCH: That is more than a possibility. I am, at least, sure though that he holds crucial information to this case.

> (Reflective music moves things along.)

> (We hear TRENCH walk along the hotel corridors.)

TRENCH: Donny Davies' room – hang on, the doors slightly ajar. I find it's always better to listen first and knock later…

DONNY: Yes, I know – as I've already said, before we go national on this secret stalker business I wanted my client to be visibly stalked or whatever stalkers do, but I don't want her killed, you raving lunatic.

> (There is a shuffle at the door and TRENCH falls in.)

TRENCH: Ouch. Sorry just trying to knock.

DONNY: I have to go – we'll speak later.

> (DONNY replaces the telephone receiver.)

DONNY: Ah, Trench – what can I do for you? I've just heard about that terrible business at the theatre. Shocking, isn't it? Poor Darnia might have…

TRENCH: …died, yes – but that, Donny Davies would have generated an awful amount of publicity. And they say all publicity is good publicity.

DONNY: That's absurd. If she's dead, I would have no superstar on my books.

TRENCH: No, but you would have something else.

DONNY: Sorry?

TRENCH: Maybe you are. We all know Darnia Storm is her public name but is it real or just a stage name?

> *(We hear DONNY rummaging through his papers and files.)*

DONNY: Yes, here it is. Darnia Storm's real name is Deidre Brown.

TRENCH: How exciting...

DONNY: And I advise you never call her that, she doesn't like it.

TRENCH: Now, isn't that surprising? Right, I'll leave you in peace. You can carry on with your telephone conversation, if you like.

DONNY: *(Says guiltily:)* Who, me?

> *(We hear TRENCH close the door firmly and walk along the corridor.)*

TRENCH: Might as well see how old Darnia's bearing up while I'm here.

> *(TRENCH knocks on the door – which opens.)*

TRENCH: Ben, what are you doing here?

BEN: My mistress requires constant protection. I will protect her.

TRENCH: Good for you. Can I have a quick word with 'mistress'?

BEN: Darnia is tired, I think it's best she rests...

DARNIA: Oh Ben, let Trench in. He is one of the people trying to help me, you great oaf.

TRENCH: Thank-you.

(TRENCH slips inside.)

TRENCH: Your bodyguard takes his job very seriously. (Then says shocked:) Darnia, what's happened to you?

DARNIA: You've never seen me like this, have you Trench? In fact, the world has never seen me like this. At least, not for a very long time...

(Music laced with sadness changes the scene.)

TRENCH: Are you sitting comfortably, Old Tom?

OLD TOM: You know only too well I am. As always I am in my trusty armchair and sitting comfortably. Your sense of irony, Trench does you no favours. Just tell me... everything.

(Mysterious music moves things along.)

OLD TOM: Describe to me, Ms Storm's most recent condition, in the hotel room.

TRENCH: Well it was like Darnia had given up. Gone was her almost arrogant sexuality; her confidence with attitude; her glowing beauty and obvious sexual charms and her 'I'm going to seduce the world and succeed' mind set. I was sad to see it all replaced by a vulnerable, scared and sad woman who seemed years older.

OLD TOM: As if Darnia has reverted back to Deidre...

TRENCH: I don't follow.

OLD TOM: The pictures I requested, please.

TRENCH: Oh, yes – here.

(TRENCH hands OLD TOM the pictures, who studies them.)

OLD TOM: These photographs confirm my suspicions.

TRENCH: Do they?

OLD TOM: I now know the identity of our mysterious stalker.

TRENCH: You do? Who, who is it?

OLD TOM: Not so fast, Trench – I want you to find out for yourself.

TRENCH: Oh, do I have to? Why can't you tell me, just this once?

OLD TOM: My purpose here is to help you; to gently push – yes, maybe sometimes shove – you in the right direction. But I will refrain from doing your job for you.

TRENCH: I knew it couldn't be that easy.

OLD TOM: Just do what I am about to say, young man, and all will become clear.

TRENCH: What do want me to do, Old Tom?

OLD TOM: On behalf of Ms Storm, I want you and Sally-Anne to invite Ms Storm herself, obviously; her bodyguard who most likely will be there anyway; the vivacious vixen Vivien Velvet and her manager, the devious Donny Davies to Ms Storm's hotel suite on the pretence of some sort of cocktail party.

TRENCH: All the suspects under one roof, eh? And then what?

OLD TOM: And then say to each one of them the following and, I fear, the secretive stalker will be finally revealed...

(Intriguing music changes scene and time.)

TRENCH: Ah, Darnia – I'm glad to see you've recaptured some of your old self.

DARNIA: Thank-you, Trench – and Sally-Anne, how nice to see you again, looking as lovely as ever.

SALLY-ANNE: Hi Darnia, but let's not start all that again.

(There is a knock at the door.)

BEN: I'll check. *(The door is opened.)* It is your manager and Vivien Velvet.

DARNIA: Who invited her?

TRENCH: I did. And now everyone's finally here, it is time to shed some light on Storm's shadowy stalker and reveal his – or her identity.

VIVIEN: How outrageous.

DONNY: Am I one of the suspects?

TRENCH: I'm going to first start with Darnia herself. Are you that desperate for attention and stardom, you arranged this whole shebang?

DARNIA: I might seek attention… but not death.

TRENCH: And you, Ben the bodyguard. Maybe you are so infatuated with your 'assignment' – you have stalked her so she will seek even greater protection – and company – from you?

BEN: My job is to protect, not threaten…

TRENCH: And the prima-donna Vivien Velvet. Are you that envious of your rival Darnia Storm, that you have resorted to attempting to inflict on her a nervous breakdown – or something worse?

VIVIEN: *(Who laughs outrageously.)* I found the idea amusing, but as I know talent will win through in the end, resorting to such skulduggery would not be necessary.

TRENCH: And finally, manager extraordinaire Donny Davies. I have heard you plotting a fake stalker – or is that a real one to give your client an unhealthy dose of sensational publicity?

DONNY: I admit I've toyed with the stalker idea, but nothing came out of it, especially not now.

SALLY-ANNE: So, everyone's innocent!

TRENCH: I don't think so – so let's start again. I'm sorry about this, Darnia but I must share your real name, which is Deidre Brown.

(VIVIEN laughs, cruelly.)

TRENCH: And those photos – of course, that's it. I can now tell you who the stalker is. *(There is a moment of expectant silence.)* The stalker and your husband, Darnia, are one of the same.

DONNY: I'm her manager. I would know if my client was married, surely?

TRENCH: Ben Brown, you are Darnia's or should I say Deidre Brown's husband – and stalker.

DARNIA: Is this true, Ben?

BEN: I'm sorry Deidre, my Deidre but yes – it is true.

DARNIA: But why Ben? You know our marriage ended years ago. Remember I only agreed to stay married on paper only, on the condition we kept it secret. I could live my own life and become the superstar, Darnia Storm – in return you could watch me from the side lines as my bodyguard.

BEN: I know the agreement, Deidre. But do you realise how hard it's been watching you change, becoming this glamorous actress and not even noticing me – me your husband. Worse, I had to stand by, helpless, while you slept with the many men – and women who either helped your career or you just simply lusted after. Yes, I stalked you, but you were never in any danger, I was very careful with the sandbag. Yes, I was the stalker, so that in some way at least, you would need your husband again.

DARNIA: Oh, Ben.

BEN: I want to be your proper husband, I don't want to be invisible anymore. I love you, Deidre Brown.

DARNIA: I've moved on, Ben. I've done so much as Darnia Storm. I don't think I could be plain old Deidre Brown again...

SALLY-ANNE: *(Who whispers:)* Come on, Trench. They're having a domestic. Let's leave them to it... Oh, and I think I belonged to the 'lusted' category.

TRENCH: Thank-you, Sally-Anne, for clearing that up for me.

(Reflective music ends the scene.)

TRENCH: So, that's when it hit me Old Tom, I suddenly realised that Ben and Deidre shared the same surname and together with those photos which showed a very young Darnia's left hand displaying a wedding ring.

OLD TOM: In the early days, she was obviously still proud to show off her wedding band.

TRENCH: And that completed the married picture and provided Ben with a moving motive for being the dreaded celebrity stalker. But you knew before seeing the pictures, how?

OLD TOM: Well naturally, when you told me of Ms Storm's real name: Deidre Brown, I put two and two together but really the clues go beyond that. Ms Storm always called her bodyguard, Ben – again like the maid in the manor-house – is quite unusual for such a supposedly formal relationship. It was Ben who brought the suspect bomb package to the person he was supposed to be protecting – sometimes the obvious clue is simply that, obvious and not a clever double-bluff. And of course, one of the poisoners pen letters, 'You must seek greater protection'. The evidence against Ben begins to add up.

TRENCH: The sandbag incident did point to Vivien though. She was actually there and had just disappeared.

OLD TOM: Ben was obviously biding his time and I couldn't really picture Miss Velvet climbing the stage gantry. Although, I grant you, Miss Velvet did have a motive albeit in an outrageous, drama-queen sort of way. Like her life, her motive was fiction.

TRENCH: And mister manager would do anything to attract publicity for Darnia.

OLD TOM: But he wouldn't do that. Davies is a cynical pro but he would had to have feelings he didn't possess to turn stalker.

TRENCH: And I now realise Ben's motive was compelling. I suppose it wouldn't be much fun to watch your wife seduce any Tom, Dick – or Harriet.

OLD TOM: Yes, as I've told you before, Trench – piece all the pieces together and the final picture becomes clear.

TRENCH: Of course, I know what Darnia meant when referring to a former lover – her husband: 'I don't see him anymore, but he's still around'. Hey, come to think of it Old Tom, you've never referred to Darnia Storm as a Miss – always a Ms.

OLD TOM: I like to keep my options open young man...

TRENCH: Do you think Ben and Darnia – or is that Deidre? – will ever be a proper married couple in the fullness of time?

OLD TOM: That is one mystery, even the Armchair Detective, will be unable to solve...

(They both laugh good-heartedly.)

OLD TOM: Trench, did you bring that pack of biscuits I asked you for?

TRENCH: Yes, here they are. Shall we have one now?

OLD TOM: Don't be ridiculous. I will open them in two years' time, when they've well and truly gone off!

TRENCH: I'll have to wait then.

OLD TOM: Oh, and I nearly forgot, there was of course one peripheral clue which pointed me in the right direction.

TRENCH: You'll have to explain, old timer.

OLD TOM: Ben said he was the best bodyguard outside Chicago. Strange thing to say, don't you think?

TRENCH: Yes, but..?

OLD TOM: It was possibly a subliminal nod to the musical, 'Chicago'; which features a starlet called Roxy who treats her husband with contempt. He feels invisible and even sings the number, 'Mister Cellophane' - sound familiar?

TRENCH: I didn't realise you were fond of musicals, Old Tom?

OLD TOM: Don't worry, I'm not about to burst into song, if that's what you mean.

(TRENCH laughs.)

CLOSING MYSTERY MUSIC

THE
ARMCHAIR
DETECTIVE

On

Holiday

INTRODUCTION

TRENCH'S HOLIDAY CHECKLIST:
(for a visit to the sleepy coastal village of Fisherman's Cove)

TOOTHBRUSH - CHECK
BUCKET & SPADE - CHECK (I'll need to do some digging.)
MYSTERY - CHECK (An enduring fifty year-old one: whatever happened to the brothers Quinn?)
GIRLFRIEND - NOT EXACTLY (But Sally-Anne's coming along.)
ARMCHAIR - AFRAID NOT (Sorry Old Tom, but it won't fit in the suitcase.)

One of my favourites of the series, as this one finally gets Trench and Sally-Anne well out of Stokeham on a (kind of) holiday. I liked the idea of throwing a challenging investigation at the regulars. Can they really solve a fifty year-old mystery, where others have failed?

CAST LIST

TRENCH

OLD TOM

SALLY-ANNE

EDITOR LAW

GEOFFREY

SARAH

CONSTANCE

MAD JACK

OLD MAN

ACT ONE

OLD TOM: Good morning, Trench.

TRENCH: Hello Old Tom.

OLD TOM: Well, sit down young man; you're making the place look untidy.

TRENCH: Now, that would be difficult.

    (We hear TRENCH sit down. There is a moment of silence.)

OLD TOM: Am I right in assuming there is a purpose to your visit – or are we going to stare at each other in silence all day?

TRENCH: No, I've come to tell you I'm going away for a while.

OLD TOM: On a holiday?

TRENCH: Actually, more of a working holiday. There is a Local Newspaper conference in the Cornish coastal village of Fisherman's Cove. Unsurprisingly it is primarily a fishing community. The place itself is supposed to be rather quaint but it's virtually devoid of tourism. In fact, the meeting is taking place at the only hotel in the resort: The Sandy Star – which has only modest conference facilities.

OLD TOM: And who is accompanying you on this jolly jaunt?

TRENCH: Sally-Anne and the one and only Editor Law.

OLD TOM: Right, Trench – in view of our recent chat, I want you to answer the next question very carefully: Is this the only reason you have visited me – to tell me about a holiday?

TRENCH: Of course not – what do you take me for, a simpleton? Tell you what, don't answer that. I also wanted to ask you if you'd like a holiday present – and to show you this.

(We hear TRENCH slap a newspaper next to OLD TOM's armchair.)

TRENCH: It's a current edition of Fisherman's Cove and district's local paper.

OLD TOM: I can see that.

TRENCH: Read the story I've highlighted.

OLD TOM: I already have. 'It is the fiftieth anniversary of one of the region's most enduring mysteries. Fifty years ago today, at first light, the brothers Quinn, instead of going fishing, uncharacteristically took a stroll on Fisherman's Cove beach. See photograph. The brothers were never seen again. Despite an extensive investigation by police and, in fact, the whole community – they never turned up. No bodies. No clues. No nothing. The Quinn brothers simply vanished into thin air. The family distraught, the police baffled.'

TRENCH: Look at the picture; it was taken on the actual morning of the disappearance – on the beach!

OLD TOM: I already have. How strange, for men about to miss out on their daily fishing trip – they are, curiously, dressed up in their full fishing gear.

TRENCH: I thought I would look it into while I'm there. Which, finally brings me to the point of my visit: can I have your 'phone number in case I need your help? Which is probably very likely.

(We hear OLD TOM scribble something down.)

TRENCH: Oh good, you're writing it down already.

OLD TOM: No, no – that's just a note to myself. I'm afraid my telephone does not take incoming calls. Although I absolutely detest them, you may give me your mobile telephone number.

TRENCH: All right, you can have one of my cards.

OLD TOM: I'll reach over for it.

TRENCH: Damn I've dropped it – hah, here it is. Blooming heck Old Tom, you very nearly left your armchair then!

OLD TOM: And in the confusion I, at least, have your number. The tea is cooling down in the kitchen; you may fetch it soon, if you like.

TRENCH: Yes, I'll join you in a brew – a cold brew.

OLD TOM: Oh and when you do go on holiday, don't forget your bucket and spade.

TRENCH: So I can build a few sandcastles?

OLD TOM: No, so you can do some digging…

(Mysterious music changes scene, time and place.)

(We can hear the seagulls; the sea-breeze; the waves crashing on the rocks and the sands – and TRENCH and SALLY-ANNE's footsteps as they walk along the beach.)

TRENCH: Stop right there, Sally-Anne.

SALLY-ANNE: *(She stops.)* What now?

TRENCH: Just let me check the photograph. Yes, with the small harbour in the background – yes this is the exact spot, well more or less, that the brothers Quinn disappeared from, fifty years ago. Err, Sall – why are you looking up at the sky?

SALLY-ANNE: Isn't it obvious, Trenchy? I'm just waiting for the aliens to abduct us as well.

TRENCH: Ruling that marvellous idea out – for now, I wonder what did happen to our fisherman friends?

SALLY-ANNE: Most probably they walked inland. Either side of the bay is guarded by those sheer cliffs.

TRENCH: But there were never any sightings of them – in Fisherman's Cove.

SALLY-ANNE: This is a very sleepy village, Trench – perhaps they were all asleep! What if they fancied a sail or a spot of fishing and set off from the harbour?

TRENCH: As you can see from the photo', the sea was too far out for that possibility.

SALLY-ANNE: The tide could have been on the turn, though. Are the brothers' families still around?

TRENCH: I think so, I'll have to check.

SALLY-ANNE: Oh, come on Trench. You've left Old Tom now. Is there really any point in pursuing such a gloriously irrelevant mystery that even Sherlock Holmes himself would struggle with? We're at the seaside together in Fisherman's Cove. If I was with someone else, maybe a holiday romance would drift along the shore...

TRENCH: With one of the other delegates? I'll have to check on the talent later.

SALLY-ANNE: Can you see what I can see?

TRENCH: Yes, there is a rather small man rushing along the sands towards us.

SALLY-ANNE: Editor Law, you appear to be out of breath.

EDITOR LAW: *(Who after taking several deep breaths, finally manages to compose himself.)* I thought I'd find you two together. Come on, the conference is due to start shortly – you'll miss the opening speech, which I'm due to make – if I ever get my breath back, that is.

TRENCH: If I missed your speech boss, now that would ruin the whole holiday.

EDITOR LAW: This is not a holiday – well mostly not.

SALLY-ANNE: Let's go back to our hotel then. The Sandy Star awaits...

(Music moves things along.)

(SALLY-ANNE and TRENCH are at the hotel bar. We can hear the usual background noises: people ordering drinks and jovial conversations. They occasionally take a sip of their drinks during their conversation.)

SALLY-ANNE: How did you do it, Trench?

TRENCH: I don't know, actually. Do what, exactly?

SALLY-ANNE: Stay awake during Editor Law's speech. Your self-discipline is more than commendable.

TRENCH: Actually, the only reason I did stay awake Sall, was thinking about our little mystery.

SALLY-ANNE: I might have known.

GEOFFREY: Hi, I'm Geoffrey. Do you snorkel?

SALLY-ANNE: Hmm, as far as chat-up lines go, err Geoffrey – that one is at least original.

GEOFFREY: It wasn't a chat-up line, just a question.

TRENCH: *(Who laughs slightly.)* Good for you Geoffers. I'm Trench and my immodest colleague answers to the name of Sally-Anne.

SALLY-ANNE: Thank-you, Trench. We're representing the Stokeham Herald. And you..?

GEOFFREY: Oh, I write for the Ghoulmouth Gazette.

TRENCH: That's way down in the West Country, isn't it?

GEOFFREY: Got it. I thought your editor's speech was marvellous.

SALLY-ANNE: It was… memorable, shall we say.

GEOFFREY: The problem with these Dos is that there's no story to work on. You know, just something to pass the time – away from the conference.

TRENCH: Actually Geoffrey, we are working on a story as we speak.

GEOFFREY: Really?

SALLY-ANNE: But we couldn't possibly tell you. Giving one of our best stories to a rival newspaper kind of undermines the world of cut-throat competition we journalists pride ourselves on.

GEOFFREY: Oh come on, Sally-Anne and Trench. Even if I did 'borrow' aspects of your story, Ghoulmouth is many miles away from Stokeham – we are not exactly competing for the same market. Anyway, I might be able to help you.

SALLY-ANNE: I doubt it.

TRENCH: All right, I'll share our story with you – but first I want to clear one thing up – no, we don't go snorkelling.

SALLY-ANNE: Not ever.

GEOFFREY: Message received, accepted and understood. I do, though, if you are at all interested.

SALLY-ANNE: I thought you were interested in our story?

GEOFFREY: I am.

TRENCH: *(Says in a hushed tone, emphasising the supposed secretive nature of what he is about to say.)* Our investigations involve events that happened half a century ago on the lonely beach of Fisherman's Cove. Events concerning the mysterious and sudden disappearance of the brothers Quinn…

(Mysterious music changes scene.)

SALLY-ANNE: Right, Trenchy – conference has finished early today, so let's go – and quick.

TRENCH: What's the rush?

SALLY-ANNE: I'll tell you outside.

(TRENCH and SALLY-ANNE quickly make their way outside of the hotel.)

TRENCH: Well?

SALLY-ANNE: Good, yes – I don't think he's following us.

TRENCH: Am I missing something, Sally-Anne?

SALLY-ANNE: Not something, somebody. I just don't want 'Geoffers' around our ankles yet.

TRENCH: I see.

SALLY-ANNE: Why did you have to ask Geoffrey to join us, anyway?

TRENCH: Because of what he said. He is not a direct rival; his offer of help – and the most compelling reason of all...

SALLY-ANNE: Which is?

TRENCH: That he seems to annoy you!

SALLY-ANNE: Thanks.

TRENCH: Don't mention it. Are we going anywhere in particular, or just wandering around aimlessly?

SALLY-ANNE: Just after breakfast, one of us did a little research in Fisherman's Cove's little library.

TRENCH: And..?

SALLY-ANNE: The brothers Quinn do still have family in the village. Their younger sister, Sarah lives with her niece – the elder brother's daughter, who's the only offspring of the brood. And that's where we're going now.

TRENCH: I'm impressed.

SALLY-ANNE: I aim to please.

(Upbeat music moves time along.)

SARAH: (Her old voice frail yet firm.) Cup of tea?

TRENCH: No thanks.

SALLY-ANNE: Trench and I had one not too long ago.

TRENCH: This is a beautiful, big house Mrs..?

SARAH: Miss Sarah Quinn actually – I never married. Now, what is it you two young people want to talk to me about?

SALLY-ANNE: We are staying here, in Fisherman's Cove for a local newspaper conference at the Sandy Star, Miss Quinn.

SARAH: I am aware of the conference and please call me Sarah.

TRENCH: And Sarah, while we're here we thought we would look into your brothers' disappearance.

SARAH: But that was over fifty years ago.

SALLY-ANNE: We just want to go over it again, to see if a fresh approach might help.

SARAH: (Says dismissively:) I wish you luck then. I went through what happened that day countless times with the police. Not even a highly respected detective from Scotland Yard could find my dear brothers. So what hope do you think you have, after all this time?

TRENCH: Yes, but I have an Armchair De… Err, just an armchair.

SARAH: I have one too, so what?

SALLY-ANNE: Could you just tell us about that fateful day, Sarah? Then we can leave you in peace.

SARAH: All right then, I don't suppose it can do no harm. The day started like any other. I was, of course, a young woman in those days. As usual, I had to get up very early to make the boys' breakfast – they eat it and went on their way. Then... nothing. I never saw my brothers again.

TRENCH: Did they go fishing?

SARAH: I thought they had – after all they left wearing their full fisherman's gear. They should have gone fishing – but they did not.

SALLY-ANNE: Then what did they do, Sarah?

SARAH: They vanished. My brothers did not go fishing as they always did. To this day, I have no idea what they did.

SALLY-ANNE: As simple and as complex as that.

(We hear TRENCH rummage inside his pocket.)

TRENCH: This is the last picture taken of your brothers, Sarah – perhaps even minutes before they disappeared. Here, take a look.

SARAH: *(Who's obviously upset.)* No, no – I've seen it.

(Another person enters the room.)

CONSTANCE: What's going on here?

SALLY-ANNE: We are reporters, just taking another look at...

CONSTANCE: ...my father – and uncle's disappearance. I see. You are upsetting Aunt Sarah.

TRENCH: I am sorry..?

CONSTANCE: ...Constance.

TRENCH: Constance, we will stop at once, of course.

CONSTANCE: But you see, you must carry on. I have more reason than most to find out what happened to my father. Is that not so, Aunt Sarah..?

(Slightly disturbing music changes scene.)

SALLY-ANNE: There is one thing about hotels, one can certainly become used to being waited on – and the view of Fisherman's Cove, beautiful. Trench, why are you staring at your mobile 'phone?

TRENCH: It's about this time; I normally have a chat with Old Tom. Last time – at the manor-house, I just thought about wanting to speak to him, but now... nothing.

SALLY-ANNE: Well, you'll just have to talk to me instead. You can pretend I'm Old Tom, if you like!

TRENCH: *(Who briefly laughs.)* I do have an imagination, but not that vivid.

SALLY-ANNE: I think we are getting nowhere fast with this seaside mystery. I mean there's just nothing to go on.

TRENCH: Oh, I wouldn't say that, Sally-Anne. If your say elderly aunt was in distress, you would want to protect her – yes?

SALLY-ANNE: Where are you trying to go with this, Trenchy?

TRENCH: But young Constance insisted we carried on talking about the picture.

SALLY-ANNE: And it was the photograph that seemed to disturb Sarah more than anything...

TRENCH: And that is what I find interesting. Wait, what's this note in my pocket?

SALLY-ANNE: I don't know – what does it say?

(We hear TRENCH un-scrunch the note.)

TRENCH: 'Come to Cove's Guest House, Room 12 at 13 Angler's Avenue – alone.'

SALLY-ANNE: I'll come with you.

TRENCH: It says alone, Sally-Anne.

SALLY-ANNE: But we don't know who's it from. It could be dangerous, you could even suffer the same fate as the brothers Quinn.

TRENCH: Don't be ridiculous.

SALLY-ANNE: What are we, Trench – exactly?

TRENCH: Err, colleagues?

SALLY-ANNE: Is that all?

TRENCH: I like to think we are friends as well. All right, to put your mind at ease, I'll take Geoffrey with me. What do you think about that?

SALLY-ANNE: Wonderful.

(Light and then doom-laden music changes the scene.)

GEOFFREY: Are you sure this is it, Trench?

TRENCH: I'm afraid so, Geoffers. I've checked and re-checked the address and this is 13 Angler's Avenue.

GEOFFREY: But that can't be a guest house – its derelict, falling to bits. The only guests staying there will be rats.

TRENCH: Well it was once a guest house, I can just make out the old, creaky sign. Right, I'm going in – alone.

GEOFFREY: What about the promise you made to Sally-Anne?

TRENCH: I had my fingers crossed! Anyway, if I'm not out in ten minutes – you can come in after me. That should ensure my safety.

GEOFFREY: I don't know about that, but message received, accepted and understood.

TRENCH: And Geoffrey...

GEOFFREY: Yes?

TRENCH: Please stop saying that.

(TRENCH then knocks on the guest house front door, which promptly collapses.)

TRENCH: Oops. Now, let's see what's inside. It's rather dark in here. Ah, room 12 must be upstairs.

(TRENCH walks up the creaky staircase.)

TRENCH: This place is awful – and full of cobwebs. If there was a cleaner, I'd sack her. And I'm definitely not ever going to stay here. Well, here's room 12. I don't think anyone will be here, but I'll knock anyway. It is the polite thing to do, after all.

(We hear TRENCH tentatively knock on the door.)

OLD TOM: Come in, young man, the door is open.

(TRENCH creaks open the door and walks inside.)

TRENCH: Old Tom, what are you doing here?

OLD TOM: Young Trench, you didn't think I was going to let you have all the fun, did you?

(Mystery music indicates the end of Act One.)

ACT TWO

(We hear the usual sounds of breakfast at a hotel, such as background conversations and the rattling of crockery.)

TRENCH: Are you sure you've had quite enough breakfast, Sally-Anne?

SALLY-ANNE: It's the sea air – it gives me a healthy appetite. Anyway, I wasn't the one who stuffed three sausages on my plate, Trenchy.

TRENCH: At least I stopped short of eating a whole pig!

SALLY-ANNE: Now you're exaggerating. I assume you survived your clandestine meeting last night?

TRENCH: Yes – but you couldn't have been that worried or you wouldn't have waited until now to ask me.

SALLY-ANNE: I had the misfortune of bumping into Geoffrey at the hotel bar last thing. He said you called him from the window saying you were perfectly safe – what a shame. Geoffers didn't say much else though, so who did you meet?

TRENCH: More tea?

(TRENCH pours the tea.)

TRENCH: Hmm, lovely. Never underestimate the luxury of hot tea.

SALLY-ANNE: I think we are becoming side-tracked here – now, who did you see?

TRENCH: Old Tom himself, would you believe? Our friend is staying in a derelict guest house!

(SALLY-ANNE nearly chokes on her tea.)

TRENCH: He even had his armchair with him. Might have been a different one, though.

SALLY-ANNE: Oh come on, nobody is going to take their armchair on holiday with them, are they?

TRENCH: You don't know Old Tom.

SALLY-ANNE: And what did old Tommy say about the queer case of the Quinn brothers?

TRENCH: Well, he agreed with us on two counts: he thought it odd that Constance didn't move to protect her rather frail aunt.

SALLY-ANNE: Yes, Constance seemed to actually enjoy putting Sarah on the spot. With family friends like that, who needs enemies..?

TRENCH: And my friend was also surprised that 'Aunt Sarah' lived in such a sprawling and luxurious house with even a panoramic sea-view thrown in.

SALLY-ANNE: Trench, you are not an estate agent by any chance?

TRENCH: No – and Old Tom asked the natural question – where did she get the money from?

SALLY-ANNE: Good question – anything else?

TRENCH: Yes, the picture. He insisted on having another look at it.

SALLY-ANNE: And..?

TRENCH: Old Tom claims that everything comes back to the photograph. He thinks that there is a vital clue staring right at us.

SALLY-ANNE: A vital clue to a fifty year-old mystery. Intriguing, isn't it? But we still have conference this morning.

TRENCH: Yes, but today we finish at lunchtime – and then…

SALLY-ANNE: And then..?

TRENCH: And then I think it's time we had a good old wander around Fisherman's Cove.

          (Mysterious music ends the scene.)

          (TRENCH and GEOFFREY are walking through the village. We hear seagulls and the odd car drive by.)

GEOFFREY: I thought today's conference was really interesting.

TRENCH: You did? You really did? Yes, you would have done, Geoffrey.

GEOFFREY: I think having a stroll through this quaint village is a super idea too though.

TRENCH: Good-oh. I thought Sally-Anne was joining us?

GEOFFREY: So did I, Trench – so did I. In fact, Sally of the Anne seemed to be coming to meet you, when she saw me and then walked in the opposite direction. I wonder why that was.

TRENCH: I wonder... oh yes, she must have err forgotten something from the hotel.

GEOFFREY: But she was walking away from The Sandy Star.

TRENCH: Never mind that. Oh, by the way Geoffers – I wouldn't mention 'Sally of the Anne' to her face – she hates it.

GEOFFREY: Message received, accepted...

TRENCH: ...and understood – yes, I know. Right, from this vantage point we can see a few things.

GEOFFREY: The harbour, the beach where you-know-who went God-knows-where.

TRENCH: That's actually quite good, Geoffrey.

GEOFFREY: The adjoining headland; the forbidding grey sea. And turning round: the village of Fisherman's Cove. I can make out the church, the local public house with The Sandy Star hotel in the background.

TRENCH: Geoffers, have I ever told you that you'd make a wonderful tour-guide!

GEOFFREY: No you haven't – but I make an even better journalist.

TRENCH: *(Says quietly:)* And modest too. *(Then normally:)* If you say so.

GEOFFREY: So, where to now, boss? – in our efforts to find the Quinn brothers.

TRENCH: I don't think we are actually going to find them. Hide-and-seek games don't usually last fifty years! But we might come across people who knew them – and what better place to start than the pub.

GEOFFREY: Lead on Mac Duff.

TRENCH: Geoffrey, have I ever told you..? No, never mind.

          (A brief interlude of music passes a bit of time.)

          (We hear GEOFFREY and TRENCH open the double-doors to the pub and then hear all the usual pub-type background noises inside.)

TRENCH: You get the drinks in, Geoffers – I'll have a pint of the local ale.

GEOFFREY: Righto. *(He goes to the bar.)*

TRENCH: And now to find someone who's old enough to have possibly known the missing siblings. Ah - excuse me sir.

OLD MAN: Yes, young man.

TRENCH: *(Says quietly:)* Now, who does that remind me of? *(Then talks loudly, in case the old man is hard-of-hearing.)* Hello, I'm a journalist trying to take another look at the vanishing Quinns. May I ask if you knew them?

OLD MAN: Before my time.

TRENCH: *(Says with incredulity:)* Really?

OLD MAN: You see, I only moved down here a mere twenty years ago.

TRENCH: That explains why you didn't know them then. Well, thank-you for your time.

OLD MAN: You want Mad Jack.

TRENCH: I do?

OLD MAN: Yes, he was the brothers' best friend – and went fishing with them every day, I believe.

TRENCH: And where can I find this Mad Jack?

OLD MAN: Oh, he's over there in the corner. He's the one staring into space. Legend has it; old Mad Jack's been like that since the day of the fisherman's disappearance. He still speaks though - sometimes.

TRENCH: Thanks, I'll buy you a pint when you've finished that one.

OLD MAN: Obliged.

GEOFFREY: Drinks, as requested.

TRENCH: You do have your good points, Geoffrey. Now, that gentleman over there, known as Mad Jack, actually knew the Quinn brothers. But as he looks a bit... a bit...

GEOFFREY: ...mad?

TRENCH: Err, eccentrically challenged. We must tread very carefully, with great subtlety.

(We hear them walk over to MAD JACK.)

GEOFFREY: Greetings Mad Jack. You knew the brothers Quinn before they vanished in a puff of smoke, did you not?

TRENCH: *(Says slightly quietly:)* Geoffrey, what did I say about being careful and subtle? This old sea-merchant isn't going to respond to direct questioning like that.

MAD JACK: That is so, me lad Geoff. I admire plain speaking. I knew the Quinns p'haps better than anyone else – and was prob'ly the last person to see them alive. Truth be told, never really got over it – that's why I stare a lot – stare with real madness in thyne eyes.

TRENCH: *(Says more quietly to GEOFFREY:)* Well played, Geoffers – your 'subtle' approach worked. *(And then says more loudly:)* You think the brothers are dead then, err Mad Jack?

(The only response to TRENCH is silence.)

TRENCH: *(Says quietly again:)* You ask him, I don't think Mad Jack is speaking to me, for some reason.

GEOFFREY: Jack, looking back, have you any idea at all, what happened to your fellow fisherman?

MAD JACK: Smuggling – the brothers were up to their necks in it.

TRENCH: I suppose we can't have a Cornish fishing village mystery without it involving smuggling!

GEOFFREY: What type of smuggling? Oh, as you must have gathered from Trench's mutterings, I'm Geoffrey – and this is err Trench.

MAD JACK: I salute you Geoffrey. They smuggled the usual - I sometimes helped them – cigarettes and alcohol mostly. But, the day my friends disappeared all those years age…

TRENCH: Fifty to be exact. Sorry, just trying to join in.

MAD JACK: …yes, on that fateful day something different happened – not the usual smuggling or fishing even.

GEOFFREY: What happened?

MAD JACK: I'm getting to that. The brothers picked up somethin' on the sea-wireless. A ship on its way back from Africa, The Schooner, had just sunk near the Fisherman's Cove headland.

TRENCH: Did they go to help the survivors? Sorry, you ask him Geoffrey.

GEOFFREY: Did they..?

MAD JACK: Not exactly. Apart from being fine fisherman, the Quinn brothers were accomplished divers – I think they went to search the wreck.

GEOFFREY: And what did they find, Mad Jack?

MAD JACK: I wouldn't know – but I believe whatever it was cost them their lives. I nearly went with 'em – and that's what has always disturbed me. That's why I stare a lot – stare with real madness in thyne eyes. I could've suffered the same fate as the brothers Quinn...

    (Doom-laden music changes scene and mood.)

    (We hear TRENCH walk along a village street.)

SALLY-ANNE: *(Who shouts:)* Trench! Trench, over here.

TRENCH: Got you, Sally.

    (TRENCH walks over to meet SALLY-ANNE.)

SALLY-ANNE: Fancy meeting you here.

TRENCH: Hmm, yes. It's odd you suddenly turn up just after Geoffrey has left to return to the hotel.

SALLY-ANNE: A pure coincidence.

TRENCH: You don't like Geoffrey, do you?

172

SALLY-ANNE: It's not that I don't like him – it's just that I can't stand him. I don't know. He just irritates the hell out of me, I suppose.

TRENCH: Well Sally-Anne, I have some great news for you then.

SALLY-ANNE: Has Geoffrey disappeared and the brothers Quinn turned up in some sort of bizarre swap?

TRENCH: You can be very cruel sometimes. After speaking to Mad Jack, an old buddy of the Quinns, we've discovered – well Geoffrey did because for some reason, Mad Jack wouldn't speak to me.

SALLY-ANNE: Trench, I'm starting to get that sinking feeling so just tell me.

TRENCH: All right. Fifty years ago, 'The Schooner' returning from Africa, and had that sinking feeling supposedly just near that headland.

SALLY-ANNE: You're kidding – you're not kidding.

TRENCH: Mad Jack has loaned us his boat from the harbour – and we're going on a little boat trip.

SALLY-ANNE: And where does Geoffrey come into all this?

TRENCH: He's helpfully gone to fetch his snorkelling gear – and wet suit. Geoffers is going to search the wreck.

SALLY-ANNE: I suppose it's my own fault for asking. Do you think he'll find the brother's remains down there?

TRENCH: Stranger things have been uncovered on the sea bed but... Wait, there's Constance – quick let's cross the road.

(TRENCH and SALLY-ANNE dash across the road.)

TRENCH: Constance.

CONSTANCE: Hello again.

SALLY-ANNE: That's a very smart outfit you're wearing. *(Then adds more quietly:)* And expensive.

CONSTANCE: What are you trying to say?

TRENCH: To put it bluntly, we were wondering where your obvious wealth comes from.

CONSTANCE: My allowance comes from Aunt Sarah.

SALLY-ANNE: All right Constance – and where did Aunt Sarah inherit or receive all this money? If you don't mind me asking.

TRENCH: Win on the lottery, was it?

CONSTANCE: Do you really think I would tell complete strangers of intimate family secrets – and upset my Aunt Sarah, the person who brought me up, even more than you already have done?

SALLY-ANNE: What happened to your mother?

CONSTANCE: She died giving birth to me. Now, any more intrusive questions, or can I go?

TRENCH: Well...

CONSTANCE: I was only eight when my father and uncle vanished – now I'm nearly sixty – and yes, I will answer even if it does upset Aunt Sarah, because I must find out what happened. I want to find out...

   (Solemn music changes the scene and time.)

   (We can hear the choppy waters of the sea, as the rowing-boat that TRENCH and SALLY-ANNE are on, is clearly rocking.)

SALLY-ANNE: He's been down there a long time.

TRENCH: Worrying about Geoffers, are we Sally-Anne?

SALLY-ANNE: It's freezing on this boat – I just want to get out of here.

TRENCH: The trouble with you, Sall, is that you don't appreciate your surroundings. Look at the view of the headland – isn't it truly..?

SALLY-ANNE: There, Trench – that was a definite tug on the air-line.

TRENCH: I think Geoffrey is ready to come up. Come on –pull.

(We hear plenty of effort as TRENCH and SALLY-ANNE pull on the rope and then splashes, as GEOFFREY emerges from the sea.)

SALLY-ANNE: The Creature from the Black Lagoon surfaces. Hello Geoffrey.

TRENCH: Here, let me give you a hand.

(TRENCH bungles GEOFFREY on board.)

TRENCH: Well Geoffers, did you find the wreck of The Schooner?

GEOFFREY: Yes, yes I did.

SALLY-ANNE: And..?

GEOFFREY: There's not much left of the ship now, but I did find something.

TRENCH: We're listening, Geoffrey.

GEOFFREY: Deep within the hull – I found this!

(We hear GEOFFREY reach over the side of the boat and pull something out of the sea.)

SALLY-ANNE: A safe!

GEOFFREY: All we need to do now is crack it open.

TRENCH: And then, maybe, we can find a real clue to this cryptic, Cornish conundrum...

(Thought-provoking music ends the scene.)

OLD TOM: Your tea should be cold enough by now, Trench. You may drink it.

TRENCH: You are very kind, Old Tom.

OLD TOM: How is it?

TRENCH: Stone cold. Just right, I suppose. Your armchair is actually a lighter brown – it is a different one?

OLD TOM: Correct. We all have to make sacrifices on holiday, Trenchy. And besides, it wouldn't fit in my suitcase! Here, I'll pass you one of my soft biscuits.

(We hear OLD TOM stretch over.)

TRENCH: Of course! That's how you gave me the note detailing this err remarkable guest house. You must have slipped it inside my pocket when you reached over for my card. And thinking about it, you crafty old devil – I bet you knocked it out of my hand on purpose to divert my attention.

OLD TOM: I am pleased to say that your deductive reasoning is improving, if only marginally.

TRENCH: I'll take that as a compliment – now where were we?

OLD TOM: We touched on the subject of Sarah Quinn's good financial fortune. Now, where did she receive such a tidy sum?

TRENCH: Belatedly Constance informed us that her Aunt Sarah eventually received it from an insurance policy following on from her beloved brothers' disappearance.

OLD TOM: Now that just doesn't ring true.

TRENCH: Yes, polices only usually pay out on proof of death – but it's been such a long time, they have probably been legally declared dead a while ago.

OLD TOM: It's not that, young man – it's more the apparent size of the settlement – and the hotel you are staying at, 'The Sandy Star'. An unusual name, don't you think?

TRENCH: If you say so – and what about the old brothers' fisherman's friend: Mad Jack? You know he's that odd, he wouldn't even speak to me – only Geoffrey.

OLD TOM: Intelligent fellow, I'd say.

TRENCH: Ouch! But Mad Jack admitted that he's never been the same since the Quinn's vanishing act. Now, is that because he killed them? Has his guilt consumed his mind?

OLD TOM: Madness is only a shipwreck away? A disturbing possibility...

TRENCH: And what was the sunken ship, The Schooner carrying in that empty safe, as we discovered later?

OLD TOM: Now, I think young Geoffrey could help you out there.

TRENCH: Geoffrey, really? He has already – diving down to fetch the thing. I think though that there must be a smuggling connection, somehow.

OLD TOM: Smuggling... Schooner... Sarah... Sandy Star... - there is at least a fair few 'S's connected to the strange events at Fisherman's Cove.

TRENCH: So, what now Old Tom?

OLD TOM: I still think that it all comes back to the picture – I'll take another look, if you don't mind.

(TRENCH hands OLD TOM the photograph.)

OLD TOM: To solve this mystery, we need to discover the third person on the beach, on that fateful day fifty years ago.

TRENCH: Woe, woe, woe old fellow – you've completely lost me there. How do you know there even was another person on the beach?

OLD TOM: Look at the picture, Trench.

TRENCH: I am. There are only the brothers – two of them. There is no one else.

OLD TOM: Now, who do you think took the photograph?

TRENCH: Of course – the critical question that has been in my hands all the time. And the even bigger mystery: why didn't I think of that?

OLD TOM: Find the third person, the person behind the camera, Trench – and then perhaps finally, we can have an answer to a question from so long ago, it has drifted into Fisherman's Cove folklore: what became of the brothers Quinn?

(Mystery music indicates the end of Act Two.)

ACT THREE

(We can hear that TRENCH and SALLY-ANNE are walking through the village of Fisherman's Cove.)

SALLY-ANNE: This morning's conference is due to start in precisely five minutes.

TRENCH: Stop worrying Sally. We'll slip in round the back. I'm sure nobody will notice.

SALLY-ANNE: That would be true, Trenchy – except that you are down to introduce one of the displays.

TRENCH: No, that can't be today.

SALLY-ANNE: It is today Trench. I know because today is the last day of the conference. I think even Editor Law might just notice your absence on this occasion.

TRENCH: Oh, I'll bluff my way through it – but that does leave us with an even greater problem.

SALLY-ANNE: Which is..?

TRENCH: We will have only one more afternoon to solve the fishy problem of Fisherman's Cove.

SALLY-ANNE: Oh that? That'll be a piece of cake compared to your absence excuse to our editor!

TRENCH: Very funny. Well, here we are – are you going to knock or am I?

SALLY-ANNE: Does it matter?

(SALLY-ANNE knocks on the front door.)

CONSTANCE: Oh, it's you – you'd better come in.

(TRENCH and SALLY-ANNE enter.)

CONSTANCE: Please sit down. (CONSTANCE then raises her voice:) Aunt Sarah, those journalists are here to speak with you again. (And then normally:) She should be down on the stair-lift shortly.

TRENCH: Actually Constance – we also wanted a quick chat with you too.

CONSTANCE: Really? I want to help, of course – but I was only eight on that terrible day. I've told you all I can remember.

SALLY-ANNE: Excuse the personal question, Constance – but you've never married, have you?

CONSTANCE: Is it that obvious? No, no I haven't – I've become the archetypal old spinster. I suppose, perhaps sadly, just like my Aunt Sarah.

TRENCH: Just not met Mr Right?

CONSTANCE: More to do with the loss of my father – and something else… For some reason, I have never wanted to stray too far from Aunt

Sarah. And before you think it, it's not the money. Although you could say, 'that's easy for me to say.'

SALLY-ANNE: Are you close to your Aunt Sarah?

CONSTANCE: No, no I'm not. I would say distant. Yes, distant is a better description for our relationship.

> (SARAH struggles in.)

SARAH: Constance, I thought I told you not to let these people in here again.

CONSTANCE: They want to find my father so, Aunt Sarah, as far as I'm concerned they can stay.

SARAH: Very well. Ask your questions and then leave. Do you really think you can discover anything new when proper detectives investigated my brothers' disappearance a lifetime ago, for months on end, and still came up with nothing?

SALLY-ANNE: Our question concerns the photograph, Miss Quinn. Take another look, please.

SARAH: No, I've seen it many times – I will not look at it again.

TRENCH: We want to know: who was the person who took the picture on that day?

SARAH: Ooh.

> (SARAH faints and crashes to the floor.)

CONSTANCE: Aunt Sarah! She's all right – no knocks of the physical kind, at least. I think perhaps you should go now though.

SALLY-ANNE: Of course, Constance – we're sorry.

CONSTANCE: Are you? I'm not.

TRENCH: And that's what I find very curious...

(Curious music ends the scene.)

(We hear the usual background noises associated with a hotel restaurant.)

SALLY-ANNE: The Sandy Star does make a lovely lunch. I'll give them that.

TRENCH: Oh, and thanks Geoffrey for stepping in and introducing that display for me.

GEOFFREY: You know me, Trench – anything I can do to help.

SALLY-ANNE: Quite. At last the endless talks and meetings are over – with only the post-conference party bash to endure – I mean enjoy tonight, and then home.

GEOFFREY: Which brings me to some rather bad news – especially for you, Sally-Anne. My editor has recalled me to the Ghoulmouth Gazette so, Sally, you won't be able to have that last dance with me, after all.

SALLY-ANNE: I'm devastated.

TRENCH: That makes finding the solution to this mystery even more urgent. So, we are all going to do an awful lot of digging this afternoon – starting now. We need to search old sea records, log books to try to find out what The Schooner was carrying in that safe.

GEOFFREY: Ah, I can help you out there.

SALLY-ANNE: *(Says with suppressed annoyance:)* Well?

GEOFFREY: The Schooner was holding a rare and expensive diamond: 'The Star of Rhodesia' – the Great Star of Africa's little sister actually. I know because I also freelance as a recovery agent for one of

London's top insurance companies. My two jobs dovetail quite nicely on this job.

SALLY-ANNE: You could have mentioned this earlier. Err, it might have helped, you know.

GEOFFREY: The information is rather sensitive – and secret. For reputation protection purposes, even the police at the time of The Schooner's sinking…

TRENCH: … and the brothers Quinn's disappearance…

GEOFFREY: … were not informed.

TRENCH: I understand totally your reticence then, Geoffrey. Thankfully, you've told us now. This changes things…

SALLY-ANNE: I'll say – and it fits in remarkably with my mornings search during the conference keynote speech.

TRENCH: The cheek! Talk about me missing a bit of the conference – you missed the actual finale. Come to think of it, I've not seen you very much in the Press Suite, particularly late morning.

SALLY-ANNE: No, and Editor Law didn't miss me either. I don't know whether that's a good or bad thing. Now, where was I? Ah yes, while the hotel manager was eavesdropping to the keynote speech, I slipped into his office and browsed through the hotel books – and discovered that the proprietor of this very hotel is none other than, Sarah Quinn.

TRENCH: Well snooped, Sally-Anne. Of course, so that's how Sarah already knew of our Press conference, so to speak. Wait, the name of the hotel, The Sandy Star.

GEOFFREY: The Star of Rhodesia.

SALLY-ANNE: Now, that is a connection.

TRENCH: Which brings the ball, or should I say diamond, firmly in Aunt Sarah's court. But we still need more... Geoffers, do you feel like going snorkelling again and diving down to The Schooner for perhaps more clues? Your friend, Mad Jack, will probably lend you his boat again. He won't even speak to me, you know. Well, Geoffrey?

GEOFFREY: Message received, accepted and understood.

TRENCH: We'll meet you on the harbour.

SALLY-ANNE: We?

TRENCH: Yes, Sally-Anne. Fancy another stroll along the beach?

('Busy' music moves things along.)

(We hear the flight of seagulls; the gusts of the wind; the waves crashing on the sands and the footprints of TRENCH and SALLY-ANNE as they walk along the beach.)

SALLY-ANNE: Of course, this could be an excuse for a romantic stroll along the beach.

TRENCH: Well, yes – and the opportunity to recreate the scene from the Quinn brothers final photograph.

SALLY-ANNE: Men... I give up. What makes you think that will help? And, anyway, haven't we done that before?

TRENCH: Humour me. Old Tom keeps saying that everything comes back to the picture.

SALLY-ANNE: Old Tom this, Old Tom that. Really Trench, you think of your precious Old Tom more than... me.

TRENCH: Come on, Sally-Anne – we are here to solve this mystery.

SALLY-ANNE: Maybe you are. All right, what do you want me to do?

184

TRENCH: I think… yes, this is the spot – let's try and exactly recreate it. You stand there pretending to be the brothers and I'll be the person taking the photograph.

SALLY-ANNE: I have one problem with this: one, I'm a sister not a brother and two, I'm singular not plural. Apart from that, I'll go with it. Actually that's two problems but let's not quibble.

TRENCH: Perfect Sally-Anne. Now, you are the first brother who's looking straight at the camera.

SALLY-ANNE: Neat idea, Trenchy – pretending the photo is the camera.

TRENCH: I know, I can study the photograph at the same time as the recreation.

SALLY-ANNE: All right, don't get big-headed.

TRENCH: Now shuffle along slightly to the next brother.

SALLY-ANNE: *(Says with a frustrating sigh of breath:)* Really. Is that OK?

TRENCH: Yes, now don't look at me but the headland. No, not the peak, look where the cliffs join the sea – yes that's it!

SALLY-ANNE: You think that's important?

TRENCH: Maybe. But it's, at least, important enough to change Geoffrey's diving plan – come on, let's see where he's up to.

        (Pacey music moves the scene on.)

        (We can hear the sea water slopping on the sides of the boats in the harbour.)

GEOFFREY: It's all arranged, Trench and Sally – Mad Jack here has kindly offered me the use of his rowing boat.

TRENCH: Thanks, Mad Jack. Err, Geoffrey – will you thank the man for me?

GEOFFREY: We appreciate the gesture, sir. Now, off to the wreck of The Schooner.

SALLY-ANNE: Oh, there's been a slight change of plan.

TRENCH: Yes, we'll be rowing to the headland, looking for a subterranean smuggler's cave.

MAD JACK: No, no – you'll be cursed like I was. Cursed with an awful madness. Cursed, I tell you.

(We hear MAD JACK run away, terrified.)

GEOFFREY: I wonder what's got into him?

SALLY-ANNE: One way of getting rid of him, I suppose. Trench, what are you looking so happy about?

TRENCH: I don't believe it. Mad Jack actually spoke to me!

(Sea-faring music moves the 'voyage' along.)

(The choppy waters can be heard, as they distantly crash on the headland.)

SALLY-ANNE: How long do you think Geoffrey will be down there, searching for this supposed cave?

TRENCH: How long is a piece of string – with a sea-knot in it?

SALLY-ANNE: I was just thinking Trench, Mad Jack is the antithesis – that's the opposite in your language – to your Old Tom.

TRENCH: In what way, Sally-Anne? Oh and thanks for the English dictionary definition.

SALLY-ANNE: Well, Mad Jack made a point of not speaking to you, whereas Oldy Tommy speaks only to you and no-one else.

TRENCH: I don't know what to say. Fascinating, truly fascinating…

(GEOFFREY bursts up out of the water.)

GEOFFREY: I've found it! I've found the cave.

TRENCH: Excellent, Geoffers.

SALLY-ANNE: Well, what's in it?

GEOFFREY: Ah, that's why I've come back – for my torch.

TRENCH: Here's your torch. How deep is it? Could you lead me down?

GEOFFREY: No problem, it's not too far down – come on.

(TRENCH strips off and dives into the water.)

(A few subterranean sounds illustrate the dive down. They swim underwater for a short while and emerge from the sea once inside the cave. GEOFFREY takes his head gear off.)

TRENCH: The cave, we've made it.

GEOFFREY: Here, you have the torch. It is your story, after all.

TRENCH: Right, I'll go on ahead.

(We hear TRENCH and GEOFFREY struggle through the narrow confines of the cave.)

GEOFFREY: Well, Trench – what can you see?

TRENCH: I… I can see it all. Geoffrey, we have finally uncovered the fifty year-old secret of Fisherman's Cove…

(Mysterious music ends the scene.)

OLD TOM: So, nearly all the elements – and I'm not just talking about the sea elements – are in place after half-a-century. You've done quite well, Trench.

TRENCH: It was you that gave me the vital clue, Old Tom. 'It all keeps coming back to the picture' – and you were proved right.

OLD TOM: Of course, the photograph also meant that something special was going to happen that day.

TRENCH: Does it? I mean, did it?

OLD TOM: Think Trench, think. Fifty years ago, photography was a lot more expensive than it is today. And could you really see ordinary fisherman having their picture taken for the usual smugglers cache of mundane contraband?

TRENCH: I see what you mean. The picture was, in a way, a celebration of the brothers' acquisition of the fabled 'Star of Rhodesia'.

OLD TOM: Yes, Trench and you know what you must do now then?

TRENCH: Go and confront the person responsible for the tragedy of the brothers Quinn.

OLD TOM: And discover the final secret: what really happened on the day fate played all the cruel cards… in the tides of time.

(Deep, reflective music sets the scene…)

SALLY-ANNE: What are you thinking?

TRENCH: I'm thinking, Sally-Anne, that I'm going to confront Mad Jack and ask him… and ask him: does my breath smell or something? Is that why he never speaks to me?

SALLY-ANNE: Shh Trench – they're coming.

CONSTANCE: The stair-lift's not working – I had to help my aunt down.

SALLY-ANNE: There's no need to apologize for it, Constance.

SARAH: I thought I had made it more than clear, crystal in fact, that I did not want to speak to you two again.

TRENCH: Crystal… or diamond? You're a star, Aunt Sarah.

SARAH: What are you talking about?

TRENCH: Sit down, Aunt Sarah.

SARAH: I am not your…

CONSTANCE: Please, do as he says.

        (CONSTANCE helps her AUNT SARAH to sit down.)

SARAH: Really, I must protest – this is all becoming increasingly insufferable, not to mention ridiculous.

TRENCH: We have found your brothers, Sarah.

SARAH: No.

CONSTANCE: My father.

SALLY-ANNE: Yes.

TRENCH: The two skeletons are remarkably well preserved in an old subterranean smugglers' cave just beneath the Fisherman's Cove headland. I believe they have been there for fifty years. And I believe that it was you, Sarah Quinn, who took that final photograph on the day of their death.

SARAH: It wasn't me, Constance – don't believe their lies. Their terrible lies...

TRENCH: Aunt Sarah, you knew they had just captured the precious Star of Rhodesia, didn't you? It was a far cry from their usual petty smuggling. You knew of the smugglers cave – you had probably been there many times. So please, end the silence – and your dark secret: tell us what really happened on that day.

SALLY-ANNE: Come on Sarah – if not for us, do it for Constance. You surely owe her that much.

CONSTANCE: Aunt Sarah, tell me... tell me... my father... you must.

(AUNT SARAH takes a heavy breath.)

SARAH: It was all a tragic accident really on what began as a special, wonderful... day. I had taken the photograph on the beach. Your father, Constance was actually holding The Star but it's hidden by a shadow. My brothers then swam to the headland with the diamond, and dived down to their secret cave. Only myself and their friend Jack knew about the cave, until now...

CONSTANCE: Go on.

SARAH: They were to hide the diamond in the cave until all the expected fuss died down – but when my brothers were in the cave, that's where everything went wrong. A storm had seemed to have whipped up from nowhere – and one of the highest tides in history, a freak event, said the weathermen – must have drowned my poor older brothers in the cave. They were accomplished divers but the currents must have been too strong to allow their escape. They must have died painfully... and slowly. Watching the water creep above their necks. Hoping for the tide to recede but, all the time, knowing and fearing the worst...

SALLY-ANNE: But you could have rescued them. You could have sent Jack or other fisherman out to help them.

TRENCH: But, maybe Sarah, you wanted The Star diamond all to yourself?

SARAH: How was I to know the high tide would kill them? They had hidden in that cave many times before – and had been safe, and even dry.

TRENCH: But you went back, didn't you? When the tide had gone out, you plucked the diamond from your dead brothers' corpses that has financed your lifestyle, ever since. Even your hotel: 'The Sandy Star'.

SARAH: Constance, I didn't know they were going to die. Please, believe me.

CONSTANCE: Your greed killed my father. Goodbye, Aunt Sarah.

SARAH: Where are you going?

CONSTANCE: Well away from you. I think I always sensed your guilt somehow. I should have left years ago.

        (CONSTANCE sweeps out and firmly closes the door behind her.)

SALLY-ANNE: Constance was always your conscience, Sarah – and now you've lost even that.

        (Music tinged with sadness closes the scene.)

        (We can hear lively music in the background and jokey conversations – the post-conference party is in full swing.)

SALLY-ANNE: I can't believe what I'm seeing – can you Trench?

TRENCH: I don't want to. Editor Law breakdancing in the middle of the dance floor. How embarrassing... or groovy. Come on, let's look away.

GEOFFREY: Great news guys – I can make the party, after all. I'm here!

SALLY-ANNE: Wonderful.

TRENCH: Put it there, Geoffers.

(We hear TRENCH and GEOFFREY slap their hands together.)

GEOFFREY: One thing, Trench – you had help with this investigation, didn't you? Was it that guy you visited in that deserted, derelict guest house?

TRENCH: I don't suppose it can do any harm. Yes, Old Tom's help was invaluable but he's a very private person so mum's the word, eh?

GEOFFREY: Message received, accepted and understood. Right, Sally-Anne we can now have that dance you've been looking forward to. Sally-Anne, where's she gone?

TRENCH: Err, I think she's powdering her nose or something...

(The lively tune slowly changes to the more familiar mystery music.)

TRENCH: 'The tides of time'. You knew about the unusually high tide, how?

OLD TOM: That's simple, Trench – whenever I go to the seaside I always take my books detailing past and future tides.

TRENCH: Why is that, in case you go for a swim?

OLD TOM: Something like that.

TRENCH: Dark brown. You are back in your dark brown armchair. Are you glad to be home, Old Tom?

OLD TOM: I suppose I am. I've never been a good traveller, really.

TRENCH: You do surprise me. Oh, one other thing: how did you know Geoffrey could help me out with the contents of 'The Schooner' safe?

OLD TOM: Pure deductive reasoning – with an added leap. Geoffrey all too quickly joined your quest for the brothers Quinn. He had already prepared his snorkelling equipment and diving skills – and rather too conveniently found The Schooner. Which all pointed to 'Geoffers' knowing initially more than he claimed.

TRENCH: And do you think Mad Jack saw the remains of the Quinn brothers?

OLD TOM: Without a doubt. In fact, I think it was seeing them in that cave – a familiar smuggling haunt for him – that pushed him over the edge. However, I believe that was many days later. Mad Jack knew nothing of the diamond and by the time he visited the cave, Sarah Quinn must have spirited The Star away.

TRENCH: Yes, and Mad Jack then thought the cave was cursed. That's why he, probably, never told the police at the time.

OLD TOM: Well summed up, dear Trench. And even the name of the Cornish village was also a clue – albeit an unintentional one.

TRENCH: Fisherman's Cove?

OLD TOM: Substitute the 'o' for an 'a'.

TRENCH: Of course, 'Fisherman's Cave'... So, did the Armchair Detective enjoy being on holiday?

OLD TOM: It had its moments. Right, I'm parched – and it's your turn to make a cup of tea.

TRENCH: Are you sure?

OLD TOM: Come on – chop, chop young man. You're not on holiday now, you know!

CLOSING MYSTERY MUSIC

THE

ARMCHAIR

DETECTIVE

and the

Psychological

Secret

INTRODUCTION

"What has turned an independent woman into a Stepford Wife?"

An old college girlfriend of Sally-Anne's has disturbingly changed since her marriage. Is her friend's controlling husband responsible?
Trench and Old Tom have plenty to think about. To help, they must uncover a frightening secret from the past...

I felt I had reached a mid-season peak with On Holiday *and wanted* The Psychological Secret *to be downbeat to further highlight the forthcoming drama of* The Last Ever Case. *Having said that, I love the way the two different plot elements mesh together so well towards the psychological climax.*

CAST LIST

TRENCH

OLD TOM

SALLY-ANNE

EDITOR LAW

GORDON

VICKY

MRS HOPKINS

HAROLD

JAMES

DAVID

TAXI DRIVER/WAITER

ACT ONE

OPENING MYSTERY MUSIC

OLD TOM: Come in, young man, the door is open.

(TRENCH goes through the usual routine of coming inside OLD TOM's flat and sitting opposite his beloved armchair.)

TRENCH: Err, how are things at the moment?

OLD TOM: Trench, is that really the reason you have come here – to ask me that?

TRENCH: No, it's just that the thing I have come to discuss with you – I'm not sure you could call it a case; a mystery; an investigation. I'm not sure it's the sort of thing we usually do together at all.

OLD TOM: Why don't you simply tell me – and then let me decide whether it is worthy of my attention?

TRENCH: All right, Old Tom, I will. That's funny, you've made two cups of tea – how did you know I was going to visit?

OLD TOM: I didn't. I sometimes make an extra cup of tea, just in case a certain reporter decides to descend on me.

TRENCH: And what happens to the tea if I don't decide to visit?

OLD TOM: I drink it. Now drink yours before it gets warm.

TRENCH: Right.

(We hear TRENCH take a few tentative sips.)

OLD TOM: How is it?

TRENCH: Cold – just how you like it.

OLD TOM: Good, now do you care to tell me what's on your mind?

TRENCH: Sally-Anne's best friend, Vicky has just got married.

OLD TOM: I would offer her my congratulations, but…

TRENCH: I know – that would involve rising from that beloved armchair of yours.

OLD TOM: And what's the problem with this marriage? Did her husband vanish on the honeymoon or something?

TRENCH: No, it's not that, Old Tom, it's – oh dear, you're not going to like this…

OLD TOM: Spit it out, Trench… I insist.

TRENCH: Well… Sally-Anne says this Vicky has changed…

OLD TOM: In what way, Trench?

TRENCH: She's just not herself anymore. Sall's Vicky was outgoing, bubbly, bright and cheerful but, according to my colleague, is now reserved, quiet, introverted and, I suppose, downright miserable. Her get up and go has got up and gone. Her husband runs a hardware store. He's called Gordon, by the way.

OLD TOM: Fascinating, absolutely fascinating…

TRENCH: There you go, I told you you wouldn't be interested. It's not really a mystery at all. I'm sorry to have bothered you with it. I'll be on my way, then.

OLD TOM: Wait. I find that sarcasm strains the sole. I meant it when I described the case as fascinating.

TRENCH: Case..?

OLD TOM: It could be the usual newly-wed blues but Vicky's condition sounds more extreme than that. What has caused her to sell her self-esteem down the proverbial river?

TRENCH: Yes, what turns a promising young woman into a 'Stepford Wife'?

OLD TOM: Apart from marriage? Yes, I think we shall investigate this… err situation. Instead of chasing stalkers and missing persons, why can't we really help someone for a change?

TRENCH: You've surprised me, Old Tom. I was ready to have my knuckles wrapped! I'll have a chat with Sally-Anne, then…

OLD TOM: You do that, young man, you do that. In fact, I think it's high time you had a nice meal in one of those new-fangled, fancy, restaurants in town. Just the four of you…

(Music to think about ends the scene.)

(We can hear the shuffling of paper and the odd punch of keys on a keyboard as TRENCH and SALLY-ANNE chat in their office.)

SALLY-ANNE: I see another shop on the high-street has fallen victim to the current shoplifting crime wave.

TRENCH: I know, terrible isn't it? Why can't you get honest thieves anymore?

SALLY-ANNE: *(Who ignores TRENCH:)* Hmm, new research claims that the average shoplifting felon is becoming increasingly younger. Kids aged ten, blah blah blah. This is rather disturbing, perhaps I'll look into it.

TRENCH: You do that, Sally-Anne.

SALLY-ANNE: With Editor Law's say-so I will. And what's 'Tiger Trenchy' going to do today? If you try really hard, you could even remove your feet from my desk.

TRENCH: I can't promise anything on my feet – they're rather comfy, but I was going to work on the apparent change in your friend, Vicky.

SALLY-ANNE: Really? It's hardly a Stokeham Herald story, though. Even so, I would like to know what has caused her personality transplant.

TRENCH: Old Tom has suggested we all go out for a meal as a foursome.

SALLY-ANNE: Old Tom, Old Tom! I can't believe you have discussed Vicky's personal problems with him. I told you in the strictest confidence.

TRENCH: Calm down, Sally-Anne. Remember, Old Tom only actually speaks to me so it's hardly likely to go any further, is it?

SALLY-ANNE: I suppose not, but I'm still not happy about it.

TRENCH: Oh cheer up. With Old Tom's bloodhound-like skills on board, we might be really able to help Vicky.

SALLY-ANNE: All right, having dinner with Vicky and Gordon might be a good idea – I'll arrange it.

TRENCH: Good. I know Gordon manages a hardware store, but what does your friend do for a living?

SALLY-ANNE: She's studying to be a lawyer at university.

TRENCH: Still?

SALLY-ANNE: Oh yes, that's one thing that won't change. Vicky is passionate about Law.

EDITOR LAW: Is she now? And I've not even met her!

     (We hear TRENCH quickly take his feet off the desk.)

TRENCH: Oops.

SALLY-ANNE: Editor Law, I didn't realise you'd come in.

EDITOR LAW: I gathered that. Surprisingly, I pay you two to uncover stories of local interest to the local populace – not just gossip about one of your friends.

TRENCH: I know, terrible isn't it?

EDITOR LAW: Or suggest dinner parties, Trench.

TRENCH: Ouch. But I am going to investigate this recent shoplifting spree. One of my better ideas, even if I say so myself.

SALLY-ANNE: Excuse me, that's my story – and idea.

EDITOR LAW: Now, let's not argue children. You can both work on the story.

TRENCH: Thank-you, Editor Law.

SALLY-ANNE: Most kind of you, Editor Law.

EDITOR LAW: But this time I want results, not excuses. I'll be in my office.

(We hear EDITOR LAW sweep out of the office.)

TRENCH: The nerve, the cheek.

SALLY-ANNE: Oh Trench, don't you dare talk to me about nerve and cheek. 'One of my better ideas', indeed.

(Quirky music changes scene.)

(We can hear the usual background noises associated with a top-class restaurant.)

WAITER: Have you decided on the wine, yet?

SALLY-ANNE: Well, that's one thing I don't have to ask Vicky about. The usual burgundy, I take it?

VICKY: (Her voice has a slightly nervous, unsure quality about it.) I used to drink burgundy – is that all right, Gordon?

GORDON: We usually drink white wine these days.

VICKY: Sorry, Sally-Anne – we'd better have white, then.

GORDON: But hey, we're with friends so let's spoil ourselves, shall we?

TRENCH: One of your finest Burgundies then, waiter.

WAITER: Understood.

(There is a moment of awkward silence.)

TRENCH: So, Gordon – how's the hardware trade, these days?

GORDON: I can't complain, Trench. Well I could, but it wouldn't do any good.

(GORDON laughs at his own little joke, but then waits for the others to laugh. There is no laughter for a moment until VICKY dutifully, joins in with a somewhat forced chuckle.)

GORDON: Thank-you, my dear – it wasn't that funny. Profits are up in the shop, actually.

SALLY-ANNE: So, how you've managed that? Done a 3 for 2 promotion on all lawnmowers?

GORDON: Not exactly. Control, Sally – it's all down to strict control. From the stock to carefully adjusting prices – and keeping a close eye on the goods. Control in all areas is the only way to run a business.

SALLY-ANNE: *(Says obviously bored:)* How interesting.

TRENCH: Well, I'd be extra careful if I was you, Gordon. There's a nasty spate of shoplifting running through the town – in fact it's a story we are currently investigating. So watch out, or you might be the next victim.

VICKY: Maybe you will have to limit the number of people who enter the shop, Gordon.

GORDON: Don't be ridiculous, Vicky. Sorry about this. *(He talks more quietly to VICKY but can still be clearly heard by TRENCH and SALLY-ANNE.)* What have I told you about thinking before speaking?

VICKY: Sorry, Gordon.

GORDON: Every inch of the shop floor is covered by CCTV and most of the staff are highly trained in such matters.

SALLY-ANNE: Now, why doesn't that surprise me?

WAITER: Would you like to order now?

VICKY: I'll have a...

GORDON: We'll have the soup followed by two sirloin steaks, cooked exactly medium.

SALLY-ANNE: But Vicky – you can't, you're a vegetarian.

GORDON: She was a vegetarian.

TRENCH: The same for us, Sally-Anne?

SALLY-ANNE: Don't get any ideas, Trench – but yes, I'll go with the flow.

WAITER: Understood.

VICKY: I can recommend marriage, what about you Gordon?

GORDON: Ah, but you have the advantage over me, dear wife because you are lucky enough to be married to me.

SALLY-ANNE: I think I'm going to be sick.

TRENCH: Don't be silly, Sally – you've not eaten yet.

SALLY-ANNE: No, but I think I've had more than I can stomach.

TRENCH: Hah – ignore us. Sally-Anne's has always had an awfully strange sense of humour.

GORDON: And, have you two any plans to tie the knot?

VICKY: Oh Gordon, didn't you know they're not an item?

GORDON: Of course dear. I was, what is known as, teasing.

TRENCH: To clear up the confusion: Sally-Anne and I are just good friends.

SALLY-ANNE: And how's the degree going on, Vicky? You must be near your finals by now.

(There is another awkward silence.)

VICKY: Err… fine.

SALLY-ANNE: Hey, Vicky – remember after college when we used to hang about the chip shop, and that lad from the science block, I think – went and dropped his…

(VICKY laughs slightly, but stops abruptly when GORDON speaks.)

GORDON: We don't talk about the old days, do we Vicky?

VICKY: Oh, no. Gordon and I like to focus on the future, because…

TRENCH: The future is bright?

SALLY-ANNE: The future's married…

(Music with a disturbing edge closes the scene.)

(We can hear the taxi-cab engine running which then stops. A cab door is opened.)

TRENCH: Goodbye then. It was an… err pleasant evening.

SALLY-ANNE: And Vicky, we must go out alone sometime, just like the old days.

GORDON: We will see.

TAXI DRIVER: Hurry up will yer, I'm only a humble cabbie – I do have other fares to collect tonight.

VICKY: Bye, sorry.

(The door is closed and the taxi drives off. TRENCH and SALLY-ANNE remain inside the taxi.)

TRENCH: East side of Stokeham, now driver.

TAXI DRIVER: Gotcha.

SALLY-ANNE: I hate him, I hate him, I hate him! I could cheerfully kill him without any guilt whatsoever.

TRENCH: Oh, come on, Sally-Anne. I don't think Editor Law is that bad – not really.

SALLY-ANNE: You know very well I was referring to Gordon – Gordon the control freak. He as good as tells her what she can drink and eat. I mean, she's suddenly not even a veggie.

TRENCH: People do sometimes change their minds.

SALLY-ANNE: And she should change her husband because he has changed her.

TRENCH: Yes, and from what you had previously told me about Vicky – seeing her in person – she has obviously undergone a remarkable transformation. But why?

SALLY-ANNE: Well it's him. It's as if he's almost shut off Vicky's old life completely and pulls all her strings.

TRENCH: But why has Gordon all but destroyed her? Turned vibrant Vicky into Vicky the victim?

SALLY-ANNE: As I've said, he's a control freak, Trench. A dominating force studying law has become a… dormant doormat.

TRENCH: But, at least, she still is a Law Student.

SALLY-ANNE: Is she, I wonder..?

             (The taxi stops.)

TAIX DRIVER: Time for you two love birds to return to your nest?

TRENCH: A-hem.

SALLY-ANNE: Don't even go there – and besides I'm not in the mood.

             (Quirky and then thoughtful music ends the scene.)

OLD TOM: So, Trench, you and Sally-Anne dined with Vicky and Gordon, and then dropped them off from the taxi. What happened after that?

TRENCH: After some confusion, I escorted Sally-Anne to her door and then the taxi driver was good enough to take me home. Once I was in my house, I went straight upstairs to brush my teeth; then I put my pyjamas on and...

OLD TOM: I don't want a running commentary to that extent, young man. I'm not that interested. I want to know what you have done the day after the meal – that's today, by the way.

TRENCH: Well, I...

OLD TOM: Edited highlights only, please. One day I might surprise you and get up from this armchair and clout you one!

TRENCH: All right, keep your grey hair on.

OLD TOM: No, let me see if I can accurately deduct your activities.

TRENCH: Old Tom, I give up.

OLD TOM: Right, this morning, seeing as you're investigating the Stokeham shoplifting spree, you probably visited the high-street shopping area. I imagine you would have spent most of the morning trying to gather information. That was, most likely, followed by a light luncheon with Sally-Anne. After that, you both managed to pluck up enough courage to visit Gordon's hardware store on the pretence of covering the shoplifting story.

TRENCH: Old Tom, I'm speechless. How could you possibly..?

OLD TOM: First, contrary to popular belief, I can actually read. I am aware of the shop-thefts from none other than the Stokeham Herald.

TRENCH: Fair enough, but what about lunch?

OLD TOM: It's a bit late for that now, don't you think?

TRENCH: Not now! I mean how did you know I had a mid-day snack with Sally?

OLD TOM: Supposition. You journalists never let an opportunity of some food slip by, especially when it's on expenses. The lovely Sally-Anne is your partner, professionally speaking of course, so it's easy to presume you lunched with her.

TRENCH: 'You presume a lot, Mr Bond.' Sorry, must stop watching those films.

OLD TOM: And as for visiting the hardware store, even I wouldn't have been able to resist that one. Such a handy excuse...

TRENCH: All that talk about food and lunch has made me feel rather peckish...

OLD TOM: There is some cake in the tin next to you. Help yourself.

TRENCH: I will, thanks.

(We hear TRENCH open the tin and happily munch on the cakes.)

TRENCH: These are quite scrumptious, actually. Even though they're slightly stale.

OLD TOM: They are nice. Pass me one when you're finished.

TRENCH: Oh, sorry – I've eat both of them. I didn't realise...

OLD TOM: Journalists. Take that cake out of its wrapper – on your other side and put it in the tin.

(We hear TRENCH follow OLD TOM's command.)

TRENCH: Here you are, then.

OLD TOM: Oh no, that cake is far too fresh. I'll have to wait a good few months before I can eat it. No matter – did you unearth any useful information from Gordon at his DIY establishment?

TRENCH: Not really. All he did was describe in excruciating, boring detail his highly elaborate anti-theft devices to put-off would be pilferers.

OLD TOM: Was he... err wearing anything unusual?

TRENCH: The usual, bog-standard long brown overall like the rest of this staff – but wait, he did have it open. Yes, he was wearing a bright red belt. I thought it was odd at the time. It just didn't go with the rest of his mundane clothes.

OLD TOM: That could be interesting, Trench.

TRENCH: So, what should I do – call the fashion police?

OLD TOM: Well, we now know the cause of dear Vicky's abrupt change of personality.

TRENCH: We do?

OLD TOM: Gordon – and his treatment of her. So now you must focus your investigation on him. Walk into his past, get inside his head. Discover why he uses his wife as a dishcloth.

TRENCH: I'll see what I can do.

OLD TOM: Oh, and catch this shoplifter while you're at it.

TRENCH: Anything else, Old Tom? Like solve all local burglaries at the same time?

OLD TOM: No, young Trench. You can go, now.

TRENCH: Bye.

(TRENCH gets up to leave.)

OLD TOM: Oh, there is one more thing.

TRENCH: Yes?

OLD TOM: You owe me some cake!

(Mystery music indicates the end of Act One.)

ACT TWO

(We can hear the traffic and the pedestrians as TRENCH and SALLY-ANNE approach the high-street shops of Stokeham.)

SALLY-ANNE: Trench, do you think we are really going to catch this shoplifter red-handed?

TRENCH: We might.

SALLY-ANNE: Oh come on – didn't we wander around the shops enough yesterday morning? It is supposed to be us girls who need this so-called retail therapy.

TRENCH: In case you hadn't noticed, Sally-Anne – I didn't actually buy anything.

SALLY-ANNE: That's even worse – the dreaded window shopper! A bargain browser who doesn't buy, err just browses.

TRENCH: All right, all right – I get the message. And the reason we're coming back at this time is because one of the shopkeepers thought the shoplifter usually seemed to strike at lunchtime.

SALLY-ANNE: Ah-ha, I detect the influence of Oldy Tom in this. Did he put you up to it?

TRENCH: Actually, no. Old Tom was in an incredibly know-it-all mood last night, even for him so I omitted to tell him the lunchtime theory. If I had tried, he probably would have still somehow told me first!

SALLY-ANNE: The shops. Are we working undercover?

TRENCH: Just get on with it.

(*Traditional detective-spy style music is played as TRENCH and SALLY-ANNE wander around the shops. As they start speaking again, the music gradually fades away.*)

SALLY-ANNE: Come on, Trenchy – this is the eighth shop I've been dragged around and there's no sign of any lifting, let alone any shops. Well, there is sign of shops – eight so far actually and shop signs of course. Stop me, by the way, if you think I'm babbling because I do...

TRENCH: Wait, I think there's a commotion in men's clothing.

SALLY-ANNE: 'nuff said! Yes, there's a bunch of youths surrounding who I think is the store detective. Shape yourself, let's have a look.

TRENCH: Heh, I wasn't the one babbling for Britain!

STORE DETECTIVE: Right, hoppit then lads, before I change my mind.

(*With a few mumbles and groans, the group of lads drift away.*)

TRENCH: Is there a problem here?

STORE DETECTIVE: Yes, on those empty rails over there should be six leather jackets but they've vanished. I thought the lads were involved but they're clean... or too clever. Well, could you see where they would have hidden those jackets?

SALLY-ANNE: No, I suppose not.

STORE DETECTIVE: Who are you, anyway?

SALLY-ANNE: I'm Sally-Anne and this is Trench. We're local reporters working on this very story.

STORE DETECTIVE: Harold, the store detective. Pleased to meet you.

TRENCH: Err Harold, when and where have the recent thefts taken place?

HAROLD: Hmm, there have been several – all around lunchtime, now I come to think of it.

SALLY-ANNE: And what days have the err offences happened?

HAROLD: Now, let me see. There was two last week on a Tuesday and Thursday – and today, of course. Thinking about it, every other week day... And so far we've lost three fake fur coats; two Armani suits and now those leather coats.

SALLY-ANNE: Well I hope he doesn't wear them all at once!

HAROLD: Quite.

TRENCH: And you've checked your CCTV footage?

HAROLD: Unfortunately no, the cameras you can see are just dummies – simply a deterrent. But after this latest escapade, I'll be urging the manager to invest in some real ones.

TRENCH: Doesn't really help much, does it?

HAROLD: Ah, James. *(He nearly shouts:)* James.

JAMES: Harold, you've not had another..?

HAROLD: Afraid so. May I introduce you to my brother, James. He works for social services and, in fact, he has one of his young charges with him.

JAMES: Yes, hello. I'm accompanying young David here.

DAVID: Hi.

TRENCH: Hello David. Yes err James – I can see you work for social services from the badge you're wearing. David not at school?

JAMES: *(Says quietly so DAVID can't hear him.)* The poor chap simply can't take school for the whole week, so I'm charged with keeping him occupied when he's not there. Single mum who works syndrome.

SALLY-ANNE: Nice bag you have there, David.

DAVID: Thanks, it's my school rucksack.

JAMES: Right, to the point of our visit. Come on David, we'd better buy that school jumper you need.

DAVID: Bye.

            (Thoughtful music changes scene.)

            (SALLY-ANNE and TRENCH are back in their office, typing away on their respective typewriters.)

TRENCH: So, what did you make of our shopping day?

SALLY-ANNE: Not much, I didn't find any bargains.

TRENCH: Did you like young David?

SALLY-ANNE: Yes, he was very sweet – for a twelve year-old. But, mind you, he did have quite a big school bag.

TRENCH: Surely you're not suggesting..?

SALLY-ANNE: And detective Harold, only he knows that the cameras don't work.

TRENCH: Have I ever told you, Sally-Anne, that you have a nasty and suspicious mind?

SALLY-ANNE: No, but thanks for the compliment.

TRENCH: Oh, when you left me in the high-street – I went and had another chat with Gordon.

SALLY-ANNE: You didn't.

TRENCH: I did. I span him a yarn about interviewing captains of industry.

SALLY-ANNE: Hah!

TRENCH: And he has agreed to speak with me.

SALLY-ANNE: Bully for you.

TRENCH: Oh, come on Sally-Anne. I am trying to help your friend, err... to find out if it was those lads who are in on this shoplifting ring.

SALLY-ANNE: Eh, have I lost the plot or something?

TRENCH: Hello Editor Law.

SALLY-ANNE: I understand.

EDITOR LAW: Hello my two favourite roving reporters.

SALLY-ANNE: We're your only two roving reporters.

EDITOR LAW: Well, you know what I mean. It's good to hear you discussing a proper story instead of chatting over a friend's love life.

TRENCH: Oh perish the thought, Editor Law. We'd never do that.

SALLY-ANNE: Well, hardly ever...

(Quirky music ends the scene.)

(We can hear the usual background sounds associated with a pub.)

TRENCH: Here's your pint, Gordon.

GORDON: Obliged.

TRENCH: Let's sit in the quiet corner.

(They sit down.)

GORDON: Tell me, Trench, do you normally conduct your interviews in a pub?

TRENCH: Put it this way, it's not that unusual.

GORDON: And what is it you want to know about this particular 'captain of industry'?

TRENCH: Oh, we'll come to that later. First, I would like to talk about general, background sort of things.

GORDON: All right, fire away then.

TRENCH: How long have you been married?

GORDON: Six months.

TRENCH: Is it a happy marriage?

GORDON: Hmm, yes – there's always a period of change though, after the honeymoon. You know, one has to adapt to accommodate the other.

TRENCH: And has Vicky adapted well?

GORDON: She has some way to go yet, but she has made some progress.

TRENCH: *(Says quietly:)* Yeah, like changing her personality. *(Then normally:)* Have you changed, err adapted?

GORDON: We all have to do our bit. Shouldn't you be writing notes? And is all this personal stuff really necessary? Shouldn't we be talking about Stokeham's flagship store, 'Gordon's DIY'?

TRENCH: We will Gordon – and as I've said this 'personal stuff' is simply background context, if you like, to place your great retail work within. And I keep my notes in here. *(He taps his forehead.)* I'll type them up later.

GORDON: *(Who sighs bad-temperedly before taking a sip of his beer.)* Is there any other 'background' information you would like?

TRENCH: Is you wife's Law degree nearing a successful conclusion?

GORDON: Here we go again. That's her department – I don't talk about it. This interview will have to end soon. I kind of would like to return to my shop before closing time.

TRENCH: Oh yes, I don't need any more background – in fact I think I think I've got too much of it! Right, let's talk about Gordon's DIY.

GORDON: That's more like it. Now, I founded the store ten years ago when I identified a gap in the...

TRENCH: That's a wonderfully different belt you're wearing. So bright, so red. Where did you buy it, if you don't mind me asking? I'm sorry, Gordon – I've interrupted your flow, haven't I?

GORDON: *(Says in a slight daze:)* It was my mother's belt.

TRENCH: Before she gave it to you?

GORDON: Before I took it from her...

(Slightly disturbing music closes the scene.)

(TRENCH is busily typing away at his computer in his office, but abruptly stops when Sally-Anne walks in.)

TRENCH: Sally-Anne, where've you been?

SALLY-ANNE: Oh, I thought I'd take a leaf out of your book.

TRENCH: In case you hadn't noticed – I'm not actually reading at the moment.

SALLY-ANNE: Hah.

TRENCH: Just trying to write this article.

SALLY-ANNE: Sorry to have disturbed you then.

TRENCH: Well, you have disturbed me – so there.

SALLY-ANNE: You've always been disturbing, Trench.

TRENCH: Listen, are you going to tell me or not?

SALLY-ANNE: I might do.

TRENCH: Hmm, Sally-Anne – have you ever suffered death by impatience?

SALLY-ANNE: Nah, I wouldn't be able to wait for it. All right, whilst you were out gallivanting with Gordon, I visited Vicky at home, knowing of course she would be alone. Hang about, I'd better talk more quietly.

TRENCH: I've lost you there.

SALLY-ANNE: Editor Law doesn't exactly approve of this line of enquiry.

TRENCH: Oh, don't worry about him – he's out playing golf all afternoon. So, did Vicky invite you in?

SALLY-ANNE: Considering her recent behaviour, yes surprisingly she did.

TRENCH: And was the tea hot?

SALLY-ANNE: Now, I don't follow you.

TRENCH: Doesn't matter, carry on.

SALLY-ANNE: Well we sat down and drunk our tea. Vicky said she couldn't chat for long as she had to soon start making a meal for Gordon.

TRENCH: And Vicky does know how to make a meal of things, doesn't she?

SALLY-ANNE: Trench, that's not funny.

TRENCH: Yeah, sorry. Did you find out anything useful?

SALLY-ANNE: Well, Vicky claims she is still at university, studying Law but I spotted a name badge near her handbag bearing the legend: 'Vicky-happy to help-Gordon's DIY'.

TRENCH: That doesn't mean she has necessarily quit her course.

SALLY-ANNE: I know, she might just be helping out part-time in holidays, that sort of thing, but it's still worrying. She still refuses to talk about what we used to laughingly call 'the old days' even though

Gordon wasn't there. As my frustration was beginning to show, she began to usher me out. So, I asked the question: Why have you so completely changed?

TRENCH: And what was her reply?

SALLY-ANNE: 'I have not changed – not one bit.'

TRENCH: Self delusional?

SALLY-ANNE: If we are to save my friend, from herself – and Gordon, we are going to have to find out the reason for Gordon's compulsive, controlling behaviour by perhaps slowly remove the layers from his personality and past.

TRENCH: I'm working on it...

        (Thoughtful music moves things on.)

        (We hear the sound of the door chime as TRENCH walks into Gordon's DIY.)

GORDON: Ah, Trench – how surprising to see you in here, again. Now, let me see, what do you want? More information on my marriage or more shoplifting scare stories?

TRENCH: Believe it or not, Gordon – I have come in here to buy something.

GORDON: My do-it-yourself store is at your tender mercies...

TRENCH: Hammers.

GORDON: Excuse me.

TRENCH: Well, hammer actually. Where are they?

GORDON: There's a selection over there.

TRENCH: Ah, this one will do.

GORDON: Do you realise you have picked the most expensive hammer we stock? It has an integrated polymer-resin compound on the head to make a very tough fellow indeed.

TRENCH: This will do then.

GORDON: I'll till it up.

FEMAIL VOICE: Do you need any help out there, Gordon?

GORDON: No dear, I mean oh dear – yes, you stay in the back stocktaking.

(We hear the till being operated and TRENCH handing over the money.)

GORDON: Anything else?

TRENCH: You don't sell belts, do you? Bright, red ones.

GORDON: No.

(A short passage of music changes scene.)

OLD TOM: Come in, young man, the door is open.

(TRENCH enters OLD TOM's flat and sits down opposite him in the living room.)

TRENCH: I've brought you a present, Old Tom.

OLD TOM: What would I do with a present? Never mind, show it to me – and I'll decide.

TRENCH: Here you are, then.

(TRENCH hands over the bag to OLD TOM.)

OLD TOM: A hammer? What would..? I suppose Trench, I could knock some sense into you! I thought you were going to give me some cake to replace what your greed consumed on your last visit.

TRENCH: Now, that's gratitude for you. It's made of a special resiny thingy, you know.

OLD TOM: I suppose it might come in useful one day.

TRENCH: That's the nearest thing I'm going to get to a thank-you, isn't it?

OLD TOM: Put it in the kitchen drawer.

TRENCH: The kitchen drawer?

OLD TOM: Yes, it'll go with the cutlery.

TRENCH: If you say so.

OLD TOM: And put the kettle on while you're there.

(TRENCH places the hammer in the cutlery drawer; puts the kettle on and returns to the living room.)

OLD TOM: Naturally, buying the hammer from the imaginatively titled, Gordon's DIY, would have given you yet another excuse to pester our friend.

TRENCH: How did..? Don't tell me. Of course, Gordon's shop is advertised on the bag.

OLD TOM: And on the price tag. Rather expensive, if you ask me.

TRENCH: Oops, sorry about that. I forgot to take it off.

OLD TOM: Evidently. Whilst you were mooching about the shops, did you make any progress on our phantom shoplifter?

TRENCH: Err, yes... and no. Actually there's not much to say on that subject.

OLD TOM: Playing your cards close to your chest on that one, Trenchy? Don't want me to steal your glory?

TRENCH: It's not that, Old Tom – well I suppose it is a bit. Do you know what I mean?

OLD TOM: All right, as long as you follow my observational deductive process. You want me to concentrate on Gordon and Vicky's personality problems. So, let's concentrate on the cause: Gordon. What else have you discovered Dr Freud?

TRENCH: Hah, yes. I think that Gordon's red belt is significant. It might be something to do with his childhood – and probably has a connection with his mother. He claimed he took it from her. Vicky, on the other hand, appears to be self-delusional, believing she hasn't changed at all since being married. And now it's questionable that she is still even pursuing her one passion: Law. I suspect that Gordon is hiding the fact that his wife may be now working for him instead, in the shop.

OLD TOM: And Gordon's behaviour towards Vicky?

TRENCH: Still as mentally controlling; bullying and abusive as ever. So, old friend, what next?

OLD TOM: You mentioned Gordon's mother. Much could be learnt from her. Find out if she's still around – and if so, visit her. Discover how and where Gordon's neurosis was nurtured.

TRENCH: Righto.

OLD TOM: We need to keep digging, young friend, keep digging to unearth Gordon's psychological secret...

TRENCH: I think I'll make the tea first though.

OLD TOM: Don't forget to boil the water again.

TRENCH: So we have to wait even longer for it to cool down. Yes, I thought so. I give up.

(Mystery music indicates the end of Act Two.)

ACT THREE

(We can hear the hustle and bustle of the high-street shops as TRENCH, once again, walks along them.)

JAMES: Err Trench, isn't it funny bumping into you, around the shops again?

TRENCH: Yes James, isn't it? I don't remember sharing my name with you.

JAMES: My youngest brother Harold let your name slip, I'm afraid.

TRENCH: No David with you today?

JAMES: I only look after David on days beginning with 'T'.

TRENCH: Today and tomorrow?

JAMES: Tuesdays and Thursdays.

TRENCH: I'm working on a story involving the recent spate of shoplifting that's inflicting the high-street. Have you noticed anything suspicious on your shopping trips with David?

JAMES: Oh, I don't drag David around the shops every day I have him. But when I have browsed through the retail outlets, I can't say I have seen anything remotely susp... Wait a minute, I've sometimes noticed a group of lads I don't like the look of.

TRENCH: So, attractive people are more likely not to steal?

JAMES: I'm going to have to go, Trench.

TRENCH: James, you said Harold was your youngest brother – that implies you have another one.

JAMES: Yes, there are three of us. What of it?

TRENCH: It just seems unfair, that's all. I know what you and Harold do, but not the other one.

JAMES: If you must know, he runs a wholesale distribution warehouse down the road.

TRENCH: Distributing what?

JAMES: You're very nosey, aren't you?

TRENCH: Comes from being a journalist. Occupational hazard, you see.

JAMES: Ah well, he distributes the whole range of retail merchandise ranging from shirts to screwdrivers.

TRENCH: And leather jackets..?

JAMES: *(Says angrily:)* What?

TRENCH: Oh nothing. I hope those suspicious lads keep away from Gordon's DIY tomorrow, though.

JAMES: Why?

TRENCH: I know Gordon – we go drinking together. He's refitting his CCTV cameras tomorrow, so they'll be off-line all day.

JAMES: Why are you telling me?

TRENCH: In case you and David do the shops tomorrow. If you visit Gordon's hardware store, keep your eyes open – you may catch the thief red-handed!

(Busy music moves a little bit of time along.)

SALLY-ANNE: Ah, Trench – I thought I'd find you shopping again.

TRENCH: Sally-Anne, is there anybody else I'm going to 'bump into'? I'll probably meet Old Tom himself next.

SALLY-ANNE: Now you are being silly. What have you been up to?

TRENCH: Entrapment.

SALLY-ANNE: Oh that? I've seen it. Zeta-Jonesy is in it, I think. Good ending, but I don't like the middle bit.

TRENCH: Finished?

SALLY-ANNE: Yes. Explain what you really mean, then.

TRENCH: Let's just say I've dangled an awfully large carrot in front of our chief-shoplifting suspect. So, all that's left is whether...

SALLY-ANNE: ... he takes the bait.

TRENCH: Sally-Anne, you look rather too pleased with yourself. Have you found something out, about Gordon..?

SALLY-ANNE: My contact in the town-hall has come up trumps. Gordon's mother is still alive and living in a nursing home in the outer-suburbs of Stokeham.

TRENCH: So, what are we waiting for?

(*'Investigative' music changes scene and time.*)

(*We can hear slight squeaking as the wheelchair is pushed around the nursing home gardens.*)

SALLY-ANNE: It is very good of you, Mrs Hopkins, to agree to see us.

MRS HOPKINS: Nonsense, I welcome anyone who will push me around these beautiful gardens. I'm usually stuck there, inside the so-called nursing home. I seldom have the chance...

TRENCH: ... to talk about your son, Gordon.

MRS HOPKINS: Oh yes, I'll talk about him, even to the Press.

TRENCH: Even though it might not be entirely complimentary?

MRS HOPKINS: Especially if it's not complimentary.

SALLY-ANNE: Am I right in assuming your relationship with Gordon has soured over the years?

MRS HOPKINS: You could say that. I have not met or spoken to him for nearly twenty years - which suits me.

TRENCH: And Gordon's childhood. We would love to know.

MRS HOPKINS: You can stop pushing me around.

SALLY-ANNE: Sorry.

(*The wheelchair stops.*)

MRS HOPKINS: I like the view of those trees.

SALLY-ANNE: Majestic or intimidating?

TRENCH: Must have many roots that twist and turn in the murky depths... delving through the undergrowth.

MRS HOPKINS: Twisting... murky depths... how appropriate.

SALLY-ANNE: And we are interested in Gordon's roots, Mrs Hopkins.

MRS HOPKINS: Are you sure you're from the local newspaper? Very odd line of enquiry, if you ask me.

TRENCH: Remember, we showed you our identification.

MRS HOPKINS: There's nothing wrong with my memory, sunny Jim.

                (SALLY-ANNE laughs.)

TRENCH: What was Gordon like as a child?

SALLY-ANNE: Please tell us, Mrs Hopkins.

MRS HOPKINS: Oh, very well. He was a bad boy; always crying; spoilt; selfish – and he even killed his own father, my husband.

TRENCH: What? How?

MRS HOPKINS: Even though I had told him many times not to play at the top of the stairs; he was doing just that, playing with one of his infernal cars. My husband was late for an appointment and was about to rush downstairs, when he tripped over his son – and fell to his death.

TRENCH: *(Says quietly:)* Arriving downstairs perhaps quicker than he planned...

SALLY-ANNE: How awful. You did convince Gordon though, that it wasn't his fault, just a terrible accident?

MRS HOPKINS: No, he caused his father's death. I blamed him then as I blame him now. My son became argumentative and resentful.

TRENCH: Hardly surprising.

MRS HOPKINS: But I kept him in line with my belt. I beat him into submission – and began to control my awful excuse for a son. Control his thoughts... and fears.

TRENCH: Was the belt bright red, by any chance?

MRS HOPKINS: Why yes. It would amuse me to think he still has it. A painful reminder of his deserved retribution.

SALLY-ANNE: And how did Gordon come to have the belt?

TRENCH: A birthday present?

SALLY-ANNE: *(Says quietly so only TRENCH can hear:)* Don't.

MRS HOPKINS: When the lazy so-and-so eventually did get a job at seventeen, I think, I went strike him to try to beat the memory of his father back into him – and the swine snatched my belt off me, and ran. Ran away. Never seen, or want to see him again.

            (Disturbing yet sad music ends this scene.)

            (We can hear SALLY-ANNE talking on the telephone and TRENCH typing away in the office. TRENCH taps a key particularly hard.)

TRENCH: There, I've just sent my shoplifting report to our copy-editor.

SALLY-ANNE: *(Who puts the receiver down.)* And I've just found out from university that Vicky has quit her Law degree for good. You know, I bet Gordon the controller has got her fetching and carrying for him in that grotty shop.

TRENCH: At least we now know where the origins of Gordon's bad behaviour evolved from.

SALLY-ANNE: Mummy. Whatever happened to mother's love?

TRENCH: Lost down a flight of stairs? Poor Gordon, it wasn't his fault. Maybe they should have safe parking areas for toy cars?

SALLY-ANNE: Don't think so, Trench. Daddy Hopkins simply went head over heels… into oblivion.

TRENCH: Maybe I'll leave a car or two on your side of the office. Might work on you.

SALLY-ANNE: Now, who would hold your hand if I wasn't here?

TRENCH: Old Tom.

SALLY-ANNE: And don't say Old Tom.

TRENCH: Consider it un-said.

SALLY-ANNE: There was one thing I noticed about Mrs Hopkins.

TRENCH: She's no spring chicken? *(There is no response from SALLY-ANNE.)* She's not bitter?

SALLY-ANNE: Not quite.

TRENCH: Then, prey what, Sally-Anne?

SALLY-ANNE: She never referred to her son by name – Gordon. Did you notice?

TRENCH: I noticed…

SALLY-ANNE: Probably some way of de-personalizing the loathing she so obviously feels for her only child…

(The office door is flung open.)

TRENCH: Editor Law, I must protest – you nearly woke Sally up!

GORDON: No, it's Gordon.

SALLY-ANNE: Hello Gordon.

GORDON: I have come to warn you both to stay away. Stop bothering Vicky, she is very happy.

SALLY-ANNE: Is that because you told her she's happy?

GORDON: Just keep away.

SALLY-ANNE: Nobody tells us what to do, especially in our own office. Except Editor Law of course.

TRENCH: Yes, belt up, Gordon.

(GORDON storms off, slamming the door behind him.)

TRENCH: Did you notice he was still wearing his mother's red belt?

SALLY-ANNE: I noticed...

(Thoughtful music changes scene and time.)

OLD TOM: Very interesting, Trench, very interesting. Not quite the Oedipus Complex, but there are certain similarities...

TRENCH: Maybe Gordon's mother always disliked him. Perhaps she saw him as a thorn; a barrier to her relationship with her husband.

OLD TOM: And when he died, the contempt changed into a deep, brooding hatred...

TRENCH: Manifesting itself in constant physical abuse and punishment.

OLD TOM: Which brings us back to the belt, the bright red belt that could tell a thousand nightmares...

TRENCH: And to put it bluntly, caused Gordon to become a control freak. Ruining his wife's life from his own personal wreckage.

OLD TOM: To stop this cycle of hatred, Trench, you need to confront Gordon... and break him, mentally speaking. He must be wearing the red belt though, that is the key to unlock his mind. Yes, I believe, the belt is vital.

TRENCH: I plan to have it out with Gordon this lunchtime at his own DIY shop.

OLD TOM: And while you're there, young Trench...

TRENCH: Yes?

OLD TOM: Catch those damned shoplifters while you're at it.

            (Music building suspense ends this scene and starts the next.)

            (We hear the door chime as TRENCH and SALLY-ANNE stroll into Gordon's DIY.)

GORDON: Trench, Sally-Anne – I thought I told you...

SALLY-ANNE: (Says quietly to TRENCH:) What are we going to do, Trench? Gordon's not wearing his belt.

TRENCH: Carry on regardless.

GORDON: I beg your pardon.

TRENCH: You don't beg anything or anyone, Gordon – you control, order...

SALLY-ANNE: Is that why you've turned a passionate and fiercely independent woman – my best friend, into a snivelling, subservient wreck?

GORDON: Nonsense.

TRENCH: You were not to blame for your father's death, Gordon.

GORDON: How do you know? I was to blame... Mother told me I was to blame. She beat the guilt further into me.

SALLY-ANNE: Your mother controlled you, Gordon, in a reign of terror. And now, you are doing the same to Vicky. Can't you see that?

GORDON: I would never harm Vicky.

TRENCH: Maybe not physically...

GORDON: I want you to leave.

TRENCH: Not yet, Gordon – you might need our help.

GORDON: How do you work that one out?

TRENCH: I'd keep an eye on that group of lads, especially with all this shoplifting going on.

GORDON: What?

TRENCH: Or maybe I wouldn't, because I think the lads are just a paid diversion so the real thieves can get to work.

SALLY-ANNE: I don't follow, Trench.

TRENCH: No, but young David over there sadly does. He follows his social services mentor. Hello James.

JAMES: Hi Trench. Come on David, we're going.

TRENCH: Empty your school bag out, David. Just do it.

DAVID: *(Who sighs:)* All right.

SALLY-ANNE: Screwdrivers, electric drills, tools... and sandpaper. I don't believe it.

TRENCH: Nice little racket, wasn't it James? Abusing your position in social services and manipulating a vulnerable child to do your dirty work. Of course, your brother's wholesale business came in handy – to distribute your ill-gotten gains, for a tidy profit no doubt.

SALLY-ANNE: Despicable.

TRENCH: You and your brother's activities dove-tailed quite nicely actually, but I don't think Harold, the store detective knew of your devious dealings.

JAMES: I told you to be careful, David – you stupid boy. I said this store was too risky, but you said, you said... I'm going to teach you a lesson with the leather from my belt.

> *(We hear JAMES whip his belt off and is about to strike David...)*

GORDON: No, don't.

> *(GORDON grapples with JAMES.)*

JAMES: Get off me.

GORDON: Mummy, please don't hit him. I'm sorry, I know it's my fault Daddy died. Hit me instead. *(GORDON then shouts.)* Vicky, fetch my Mummy's red belt from the stockroom – I deserve to be punished.

> *(We hear slow footsteps as VICKY approaches.)*

VICKY: I'm afraid that's not possible, my sweet. I've chopped your red belt into pieces and thrown them into the incinerator.

GORDON: It's over, finally.

VICKY: Come here, Gordon. I'll hold you. And it's an order, my order.

GORDON: Gladly.

SALLY-ANNE: And it's over for you, James – I've called the police.

TRENCH: Oh, and don't worry David, I'll put a word in for you.

SALLY-ANNE: That, Trench is what he is worried about.

(Concluding music wraps this scene up.)

TRENCH: You said the belt was vital, Old Tom – and you were proved right.

OLD TOM: Well yes, the belt was the trigger – but, of course, I was referring to the red one. Were you a bit worried when you realised Gordon wasn't wearing it?

TRENCH: Just a little bit, but fortunately the shoplifter from social services came to my rescue...

OLD TOM: ... to provide the catalyst that cut through years of cruel conditioning. And then, thankfully, Gordon finally cracked. It was just an ordinary belt that provided a link to Gordon's troubled childhood. Well, Trench – are you going to inform me of the deductive process that brought down James' robbing racket?

TRENCH: I've been looking forward to this, Old Tom. I began to be suspicious when...

OLD TOM: Hold your horses, Trenchy – first, let me see if I can piece the little information I have, together successfully.

TRENCH: I doubt it. But if you must, go on.

OLD TOM: You discovered most shoplifting incidents happened on Tuesday and Thursday lunchtimes which coincided with James' visit to the high-street with young David. A group of youths always seemed to divert attention at the time of the thefts. They were probably rewarded by our friend from the social. James also proudly and prominently displayed his social services name badge, obviously to further divert suspicion away from him. Scandalously, he used a vulnerable child, David to stash the 'swag' in his ever-so-slightly oversized school bag when no one was looking. Then he used his brother's distribution network to peddle the stolen goods. How am I doing so far?

TRENCH: I'm speechless – how could you possibly know that? You're not telepathic, are you?

                    (We hear OLD TOM throw a newspaper at TRENCH.)

OLD TOM: No, but as I've already mentioned, I can read. Reading in-between the lines of the article on the shoplifting spree in the Stokeham Herald provided me with my suppositions.

TRENCH: It's not fair, I wanted to solve the shoplifting, but – on my own.

OLD TOM: You did, young Trench – and I'm proud of you. In fact you are learning that fast, you might not need me for much longer.

TRENCH: Oh, I still need you Old Tom – I think I always will.

OLD TOM: Nothing lasts forever, Trench. When the time is right, I will move on – and so will you…

TRENCH: Well not yet, not on my watch! You'll be pleased to know that young David has been exonerated of all blame.

OLD TOM: Good. Oh, thanks for the hammer, by the way. One day, it will come in very useful…

TRENCH: Don't mention it. And Vicky is her old self again. She is re-joining her Law degree course at university next term, treating her hiatus as a 'gap' year.

OLD TOM: The legal eagle can now open her wings and begin to fly again...

TRENCH: Sally-Anne says she is now in contact with all her old friends including Sall of course. Vicky's independent spirit has returned with a vengeance and, believe it or not, she and Gordon couldn't be happier. Even though now it's Vicky who generally gives the orders and not him!

OLD TOM: So, Vicky is now wearing the trousers? Just as it should be, err I think. A happy ending, Trench – and to celebrate let's bring out my new/old cake.

TRENCH: Yes, the armchair detective has unlocked Gordon's psychological secret, I'll eat to that.

OLD TOM: Fetch the cake tin then.

              (TRENCH passes over the tin.)

OLD TOM: One for me and one for you.

TRENCH: What would happen if I took two slices?

OLD TOM: I'd think twice if I was you. If you look closely, you will notice that I am still wearing my belt...

CLOSING MYSTERY MUSIC

THE

ARMCHAIR

DETECTIVE's

Last Ever Case

INTRODUCTION

"All good things must come to an end."

Old Tom begins to realise that his time with Trench is nearly over, his work almost complete.
But first, there is their most bizarre mystery yet to solve. As new owners prepare to take over the Stokeham Herald, a strange black box sends Trench on a seemingly frantic wild goose chase throughout Stokeham. There is a rising familiarity behind all the rushing about - and Old Tom starts to sense a hidden agenda...

Could I weave together key elements of the previous five scripts; write a complete mystery in its own right - but also create a dramatic and climatic finale to the series? You decide, but if you give a wrong answer – I'll send the Black Box after you!

CAST LIST

TRENCH

OLD TOM

SALLY-ANNE

EDITOR LAW

(Cast List continued after the conclusion.)

ACT ONE

OPENING MYSTERY MUSIC

OLD TOM: Come in, young man, the door is open.

(We hear TRENCH open the front door, rummage about a bit in the hall – and then enter the living room.)

OLD TOM: It's been a long time, Trench.

(TRENCH sits himself down.)

TRENCH: Your armchair is the same as ever.

OLD TOM: As I am.

TRENCH: I've not ignored you on purpose, Old Tom. It's just that – believe it or not – I haven't come across anything for quite a while that you could help me with – until now.

OLD TOM: I'm listening.

TRENCH: Oh, this time I have a real mystery for you. It baffles me just thinking about it!

OLD TOM: I'm definitely listening now...

TRENCH: Hang on, there are two cups of tea on the table. Having not seen you for a fair old time now, how did you know to expect me?

OLD TOM: As I've no doubt told you before, young Trench, I often make you a cup of tea, as a precautionary measure, just in case you do visit. It should be cold enough by now, so drink up.

(We can hear OLD TOM and TRENCH sip their teas.)

TRENCH: As I was saying, Old Tom, about this latest mystery. It's truly bizarre, it really is...

OLD TOM: We will come to that all in good time, my friend. First tell me, what has been going on with you in the many, many moons since your last visit?

TRENCH: Sally-Anne has a new boyfriend, Jonathan – I think his name is. She has begun to see more and more of him in London. Editor Law is spending more and more time on the golf course. Rumour has it that he'll soon be going for early retirement.

OLD TOM: Which leaves poor Trenchy all alone. I imagine it's been difficult holding the fort at the Stokeham Herald lately. Maybe that's why you haven't come to see me, you've been too busy!

TRENCH: Not exactly. When I was starting to struggle, Editor Law took on a new reporter, Dominic. We don't seem to really get on but he did come recommended from the Ghoulmouth Gazette. In fact Geoffrey, remember whom I met in Fisherman's Cove...

OLD TOM: I remember.

TRENCH: …recommended us to him.

OLD TOM: Spoken to Geoffrey then, have you?

TRENCH: No, actually – it was Dominic who mentioned
Geoffrey.

OLD TOM: I see. Well, are you going to show me what you have
dumped in my hallway?

TRENCH: How did you..?

OLD TOM: I do have ears, remember.

TRENCH: I'll go and fetch it.

             (TRENCH leaves the living room and returns with the
object.)

OLD TOM: Is that the great mystery?

TRENCH: It certainly is.

OLD TOM: A black box?

TRENCH: Yes, odd isn't it? It just appeared on my desk this
morning. It had this note sellotaped onto it. Here, have a read.

OLD TOM: 'Uncover the clues to solve the Stokeham mystery'.
How intriguing. I didn't even know there was a Stokeham mystery.

TRENCH: Neither did I. I've tried to open the box but it seems
impenetrable. Maybe it's made from the same material as the black
boxes on an aircraft.

OLD TOM: A black box… about the size of a square shoe box…
that won't open… and somehow holds the secret to a new mystery.

How utterly absorbing. Fetch me the hammer that you bought me – from the kitchen. We'll smash it open.

    (The BLACK BOX starts to speak. It clearly has an electronic voice. A whirring sound can be heard in the background when it does speak.)

BLACK BOX: Take me to the offices of Property Management Limited before sixteen hundred hours to discover your first clue.

OLD TOM: Amazing.

TRENCH: Sixteen hundred hours?

OLD TOM: That's four o'clock, Trench.

TRENCH: Oh no, that only gives me barely half-an-hour to dash across town.

OLD TOM: You had better get a move on then – and sharpish.

TRENCH: Right.

OLD TOM: And Trench, don't forget to finish your tea first – I insist.

TRENCH: Oh very well.

    (TRENCH gulps the tea down.)

TRENCH: I'll be off, but first, what do you think this is actually all about?

OLD TOM: I think it's a trail, Trench. So follow it and see where it leads.

TRENCH: I'd better dash while the trails hot, then.

OLD TOM: Oh, and Trench.

TRENCH: *(Says with frustration and urgency:)* What is it now?

OLD TOM: Don't forget your Black Box, you may actually need it.

TRENCH: Err, yeah – bye!

                 (Speedy music changes the scene.)

TRENCH: Of course, Property Management Limited, I'm at Stonebridge's company.

                 (TRENCH bursts through the door.)

JILL: Err, Trench isn't it? What are you doing here? And why are you holding a black box?

TRENCH: *(Who's obviously out of breath.)* Don't ask. Ms Jill Masterson, long time, no see.

JILL: I'm afraid Mr Stonebridge is out, assuming it is him you've come to see. Trench, what are you looking for?

TRENCH: I don't know, but I've only two minutes left!

BLACK BOX: The first clue: Use the secretary as a pointer. You have ninety seconds remaining.

TRENCH: What the hell does it mean by..? You are not pointing at anything. Come on, think Trench think. But your shoes are pointed – and there are slight scuff marks on the tips... from underneath your desk! I know this is most unorthodox Jill, but would you mind moving away from your desk?

JILL: I don't understand any of this.

TRENCH: *(Who raises his voice.)* Just do it!

JILL: *(Affronted.)* Really.

(*JILL moves and TRENCH frantically scrambles underneath her desk.*)

TRENCH: I can't find anything.

BLACK BOX: Twenty seconds remaining.

TRENCH: Found it!

(*TRENCH gets up.*)

JILL: What is it?

TRENCH: A little, tiny black box. Let's see what happens if I squeeze it – it opens… There's a small black sheep inside.

JILL: Ah, cute.

TRENCH: It's getting hot. Ouch.

(*TRENCH drops it.*)

BLACK BOX: One second remaining…

(*There is a very small explosion.*)

TRENCH: How strange, there must have been a small incendiary device inside the sheep – to go off at the appointed time. Now, there's nothing left of my so-called first clue.

JILL: I think I preferred you before, when you were returning golf balls.

TRENCH: Sorry about all this, Jill. How are you these days? Are you still 'friends' with Sam Stonebridge?

JILL: Oh no, that all ended with that business at Mayflower Court. Our relationship now is strictly professional.

TRENCH: You might be interested to know that ex-sergeant Jenkins died soon after discovering the Mayflower flats were to remain.

JILL: Good. It gives me great pleasure knowing that the man I hold responsible for my father's death died penniless literally on top of a fortune.

TRENCH: Goodbye Jill.

          (TRENCH closes the door as he leaves.)

TRENCH: Well, at least she's not bitter and twisted!

          (The BLACK BOX whirrs into life.)

BLACK BOX: Meet contact at Stokeham Station at seventeen hundred hours.

TRENCH: Hmm 'contact'? Well, the bad news is that the station is the other side of town. The good news is I've plenty of time – a brisk walk will do. At least this box will keep me fit!

          (Music and train sounds change the scene.)

          (We can hear the busy sounds of a train station including the typically ineffectual loud speaker system.)

TRENCH: I wonder who my contact is – it could be anyone. I wouldn't know him if I fell over him – or her. Wait a minute, seventeen hundred – five o'clock. Sally-Anne's train from London is due at five. My contact must be her!

          (We hear the train pull into the station and stop. The door opens as the passengers step onto the platform.)

TRENCH: (Who shouts:) Sally-Anne! Sally-Anne, over here.

SALLY-ANNE: Trench, what are you doing here?

BLACK BOX: Contact has been made. Take me to thirteen, Primrose Avenue before seventeen hundred and thirty hours to discover your second clue.

TRENCH: We've only half-an-hour – but I know where Primrose Avenue is. If we dash, we should make it with a bit of time to spare. Where's your luggage, by the way?

SALLY-ANNE: Luckily, I left it at Jonathan's. Trench, what's going on here? And why are you carrying a black box that speaks?

TRENCH: Come on, we'll have to go. I'll explain what I can on the way.

SALLY-ANNE: I was enjoying myself in London. Going out to the theatre with Jonathan; frequenting fancy restaurants. Why have I come back to this?

TRENCH: *(Says more loudly:)* Come on!

        (Busy music moves things along.)

TRENCH: Thirteen Primrose Avenue. We've made it with five minutes to spare.

SALLY-ANNE: I'll knock, shall I?

        (SALLY-ANNE knocks on the door – which is opened after a few moments.)

TRENCH: Sawn-Off! What are you doing here?

SAWN-OFF: Visiting my mother. Hang on, what are you doing here?

MOTHER: *(Calling from the living room.)* Please invite your friends in, Cedric. You know how I love to meet your chums.

SAWN-OFF: *(Who sighs:)* Yes, mother.

TRENCH: Cedric! Cedric?

(They all walk inside and sit down in the living room.)

MOTHER: That's right – you young people sit down. In a moment, I'll make us all a nice cup of tea. Now dear, introduce your lovely friends to me.

SAWN-OFF: This is Trench and Sally...

SALLY-ANNE: ...Anne.

SAWN-OFF: Still seeing Marcus?

SALLY-ANNE: No, that fizzled out a while ago...

TRENCH: Err, how's Happy, Sawn-Off – I mean Cedric?

SAWN-OFF: In custody, I'm afraid. He's recently confessed to a series of crimes. Some of which he somehow committed when he was last detained. Don't worry though, my Brief will soon have him out again.

SALLY-ANNE: I'm so touched.

TRENCH: And Happy will be happy?

MOTHER: It warms my heart that my son looks after his staff so much.

SALLY-ANNE: Doesn't it just.

MOTHER: And it's so nice to see friends reminiscing over old times.

TRENCH: How's business in west London, Sawn- err, Cedric?

SAWN-OFF: Satisfactory. To establish authority though, I had to break a few knee-ca... ca...ca...

MOTHER: Yes dear..?

SAWN-OFF: I had to break a few err, free flowers in. You know, give some away to make a good start in my floral business.

MOTHER: So generous... You always have been.

TRENCH: Yes, unbelievable. Sorry to change the subject, but has anyone come across a very small black box?

SAWN-OFF: No, Trench – but you're holding one, why?

BLACK BOX: The second clue: Trouble can brew when left alone. You have ninety seconds remaining.

TRENCH: Of course, I'll make the tea!

SALLY-ANNE: I'll help.

            (TRENCH and SALLY-ANNE rush into the kitchen.)

TRENCH: Quick the tea pot, where is it?

SALLY-ANNE: (Who opens a cupboard.) In this cupboard. (She picks it up.) It's an old 'Brown Betty'!

TRENCH: Never mind, open it.

SALLY-ANNE: There's something inside... How odd, a small black box.

TRENCH: Squeeze it.

SALLY-ANNE: Squeeze it?

BLACK BOX: Twenty seconds remaining.

TRENCH: To open it, hurry.

SALLY-ANNE: Very well. (She squeezes it open.) It's a toy, model sports car.

TRENCH: Now, drop it.

SALLY-ANNE: This is getting more weird by the minute.

(SALLY-ANNE drops the car on the floor.)

BLACK BOX: One second remaining.

(There is a small explosion.)

SALLY-ANNE: Engine trouble?

MOTHER: (Says from the living room.) Everything all right dears?

SALLY-ANNE: Yes, wonderful. Just wonderful.

(Slightly slower music ends this scene.)

(TRENCH and SALLY-ANNE are walking along a pavement.)

TRENCH: It was so nice to see that Sawn-Off has turned over a new leaf.

SALLY-ANNE: Yeah, right.

BLACK BOX: Initiating stand-by mode. Await further instructions in due course.

SALLY-ANNE: 'Further instructions'. Arrogant little fellow, isn't he?

TRENCH: At least it means I can have a break from all this dashing about. I think I'll go back to the office. Coming?

SALLY-ANNE: No, I'm going to go home to finally freshen up. See yah.

(A brief interlude of music moves things along.)

(DOMINIC is typing away in the office of the Stokeham Herald, but pauses when TRENCH walks in. He occasionally types again during their conversation.)

TRENCH: Dominic, who's Editor Law locked himself up with, in his office?

DOMINIC: I've really no idea.

TRENCH: He looked like a bald-headed business man.

DOMINIC: *(Who sighs, obviously annoyed at being interrupted.)* I assume you're not talking about Editor Law?

TRENCH: Err no. Our editor has a full head of hair, albeit grey. There's a rumour circling around the secretaries that the meeting's about closing the Stokeham Herald down.

DOMINIC: I'm afraid them – and you have that quite wrong. Editor Law is in discussions to sell this newspaper. In that event, I'm sure things would run more or less the same.

TRENCH: I thought you didn't know who the mystery man was.

DOMINIC: I don't, Trench. But Law told me himself he's thinking of selling to someone – whether or not it was that gentleman you saw – I've really no idea.

TRENCH: Editor Law told you – really? He's not mentioned anything to me.

DOMINIC: He probably will at some point. Trench, what have you been carrying that black box for? And why have you dumped it on the desk?

TRENCH: It's connected with a story I'm working on. It's rather complicated, so I won't bore you with the details.

DOMINIC: I see. Working on an exclusive scoop, are we?

TRENCH: Not really, but it has given me the run-around. Have you been busy?

DOMINIC: I was trying to finish this article on car-parking problems in central Stokeham, before I was interrupted.

TRENCH: Carry on, don't mind me, Dominic. I wouldn't want to keep you from such a dynamic story.

DOMINIC: People still have to park their cars, Trench. It may be boring to you but you may find it is important to the general public at large.

TRENCH: Maybe, but I think most people should use the bus or better still walk – or cycle.

DOMINIC: Anything else before I try and do some more work?

TRENCH: Yes, do you like it here, Dominic? Were things more regimented at the Ghoulmouth Gazette with Geoffrey?

DOMINIC: Working here at the Stokeham Herald is more challenging. At the Gazette, I was used to being with professionals who worked damned hard – and got results.

TRENCH: *(Says just loud enough for DOMINIC to hear:)* It's a good job I'm not easily offended.

DOMINIC: Fortunately, I like challenges.

TRENCH: Good for you, Dominic, good for you. Oh, and when you've finished on your car-parking story, make a start on the obituaries. *(Then says quietly:)* Preferably your own…

        (Reflective music finishes the scene.)

TRENCH: So, Old Tom, the clues so far are a black sheep and a toy car.

OLD TOM: A toy sports car.

TRENCH: Yes, is that important?

OLD TOM: I'm not sure. So, what can we deduce from the evidence so far?

TRENCH: Hmm, we're looking for a secret institute that uses sheep to drive sports cars?

OLD TOM: Very good, Trenchy. It doesn't really seem to make sense though, does it? I see you've brought your little friend along.

TRENCH: Come along, Black Box, say hello to Uncle Tom.

      (The only response is silence.)

OLD TOM: Shy little fellow, isn't he?

TRENCH: Oh, I don't know – he soon speaks when it suits him.

OLD TOM: How are things at the office?

TRENCH: Not good. I'm not sure I like Dominic and it seems Editor Law is considering selling-up.

OLD TOM: Interesting... I assume it was Dominic who gave you that 'information'? Never mind, Trench – have a soft biscuit. You can make some tea later.

TRENCH: Why not? We don't really need the tea yet anyway, these biscuits are that soft they'd probably disintegrate on sight, at the thought of dunking them!

      (They both happily munch on their biscuits for a few moments.)

OLD TOM: And when you do eventually make the tea, Trench – try to make sure there isn't a tiny black box already in the tea-pot.

TRENCH: Yes, Old Tom.

OLD TOM: Now, let's look at the rather puzzling questions this strange mystery is asking us: What do the clues mean? Why were the clues found from people we have previously been concerned with? And how did the Black Box know Sally-Anne was coming home on the five o'clock train?

TRENCH: With all the rushing about I've been doing, I haven't had time to think. But yes, a pattern does seem to be forming…

BLACK BOX: Take me to the Stokeham Empire before twelve noon to discover your third clue.

OLD TOM: Well, at least, that gives you plenty of time to drink your tea, once you've made it – of course.

TRENCH: Yes, Old Tom. But after that, it'll be a case of: Here we go again!

        (*A longer piece of mystery music indicates the end of Act One.*)

ACT TWO

(SALLY-ANNE and TRENCH are walking quickly through the streets of Stokeham.)

SALLY-ANNE: Oh Trench, why do you have to drag me along too?

TRENCH: Come on, Sally-Anne – you know Darnia Storm is back in town to perform extra dates of her Play.

SALLY-ANNE: So?

TRENCH: So – I need you for protection.

SALLY-ANNE: You need me for protection? She was after me as well, you know.

TRENCH: Yes well, I believe in safety in numbers. The Stokeham Empire, we're here.

SALLY-ANNE: I expect your Black Box buddy will be pleased.

TRENCH: Are you pleased, Black Boxy? *(There's no response.)* I'm afraid he's incommunicado at the moment.

SALLY-ANNE: The stage door is open...

TRENCH: I assume Darnia is no longer troubled by the stalker.

SALLY-ANNE: So she won't be as concerned about security. Shall we go inside?

TRENCH: That is the general idea.

        (TRENCH and SALLY-ANNE enter the theatre.)

TRENCH: See that big star on the dressing room door?

SALLY-ANNE: Yes.

TRENCH: And the legend Darnia Storm bedazzled across it?

SALLY-ANNE: Yes.

TRENCH: This must be Ms Storm's dressing room.

SALLY-ANNE: Your powers of deduction are truly amazing, Holmes!

        (One of them knocks.)

DARNIA: Enter, please.

TRENCH: Ever get the sense of deja-vu?

SALLY-ANNE: Unfortunately, yes.

        (They enter the dressing room.)

DARNIA: Trench and the beautiful Sally-Anne, how wonderful to see you again.

TRENCH: Likewise. Err, Darnia can I ask why you are wearing just a black Basque with matching stockings and suspenders?

DARNIA: Dress rehearsal darling, dress rehearsal. Do you think I look supremely sexy in an utterly sexy sort of way?

TRENCH: Err...

SALLY-ANNE: You are an attractive woman, Darnia.

DARNIA: Ooh, come here and say that, Sally.

SALLY-ANNE: What about your husband?

DARNIA: Oh, don't worry about him. I've split from that creep for good. Come closer, Sally.

SALLY-ANNE: What about Trench?

DARNIA: He can watch... or join in. Ménage-a-trios. I adore threesomes...

(TRENCH coughs.)

DARNIA: Come on, Sally-Anne, let's just do it. You can decide whether you like it or not afterwards – but I guarantee you'll love it. You might get something out of it too, Trench.

TRENCH: I'm sure I would.

(The BLACK BOX whirrs into life.)

DARNIA: What the..? How kinky.

BLACK BOX: The third clue: Suspenders are found with suspense. You have ninety seconds remaining.

DARNIA: Excuse me, it takes me longer than that!

SALLY-ANNE: Suspenders, suspense? I don't get it.

DARNIA: You will though, darling.

TRENCH: Suspenders... found – of course! Darnia, where are your drawers?

DARNIA: You're staring at them, gorgeous.

TRENCH: No, where do you keep your smalls, suspenders – that type of thing?

DARNIA: To please some sort of perversion?

BLACK BOX: Twenty seconds remaining.

SALLY-ANNE: Quick Darnia, tell him – it's important.

DARNIA: Oh very well, over there in that drawer.

(TRENCH firmly opens the drawer and has a good rummage.)

DARNIA: I've seen it all now.

TRENCH: Found it!

DARNIA: I'm sure you have.

SALLY-ANNE: Squeeze it.

DARNIA: Pardon?

TRENCH: The tiny box opens... to reveal a screwed-up newspaper.

SALLY-ANNE: Drop it.

TRENCH: I have.

BLACK BOX: One second remaining.

(We hear the paper vanish in a puff of flames and smoke.)

TRENCH: I'd better put it out.

(*TRENCH stamps on the small fire.*)

DARNIA: You know how to dampen a girl's flame of passion, don't you?

(*Seductive music with irony closes this scene.*)

(*TRENCH and SALLY-ANNE are walking through the offices of the Stokeham Herald.*)

SALLY-ANNE: That was a close escape.

TRENCH: From the clue or Darnia?

SALLY-ANNE: Both!

TRENCH: I wonder what project Madam Darnia Storm will grace her presence with next? Maybe a film?

SALLY-ANNE: Yeah like, 'Revenge of the Rampant Nymphomaniac'.

(*They both laugh as they walk into their office, but abruptly stop laughing when they see DOMINIC there.*)

DOMINIC: What's so amusing?

TRENCH: Well, by the time we explained, Dominic…

SALLY-ANNE: … it wouldn't be funny anymore. It's known as comic timing, dear 'colleague'.

DOMINIC: So you're not going to tell me – fine. Can I ask this though, while I've been working hard on my car parking article and on three other topics, what have you two been working on all morning?

SALLY-ANNE: It's known as a story, Dominic. You know some of us do something called investigative journalism in the real world.

TRENCH: And not sat on our backsides in a cosy little office.

SALLY-ANNE: At the moment though, it's a cramped little office with three of us in it.

DOMINIC: Well, what is this supposedly big story and, Trench, why are you still carrying that ridiculous Black Box around with you?

SALLY-ANNE: Ever been to Charm School, Dominic? Was it closed?

TRENCH: Good one, Sally-Anne. Dominic, you don't need to concern yourself with things you won't understand. And don't call my Black Box ridiculous, you'll hurt his feelings!

DOMINIC: You know what I think? I think you've both been doing precisely nothing this morning. You probably woke up late – together.

SALLY-ANNE: How dare you.

DOMINIC: And all this secret story nonsense is a pathetic excuse to cover your tracks. I'll be glad when Editor Law does sell this place. Perhaps then, the new boss will sort you two out.

SALLY-ANNE: I don't think so, Dominic. Remember, we are the experienced professionals and you are the office junior.

TRENCH: Another good one. You're on form today, Sall.

(A figure pops in the office.)

EDITOR LAW: Everything all right?

DOMINIC: Err yes, we were just having a... creative discussion, that's all.

EDITOR LAW: Trench, Sally-Anne – I want you in my office, now.

TRENCH: Righto.

SALLY-ANNE: Don't work too hard, Dominic.

(TRENCH and SALLY-ANNE follow EDITOR LAW into his office and close the door.)

EDITOR LAW: Sit down.

(They sit down.)

EDITOR LAW: You've probably heard the rumours flying around but now it's all sorted, I want you two to be the first to know. I will inform the rest of the staff later today.

TRENCH: *(Asks tentatively:)* Are you selling up?

EDITOR LAW: Yes, I am selling the newspaper to a businessman, Max Sterling. You may have seen me having a meeting with him yesterday.

TRENCH: Bald headed guy in a suit?

EDITOR LAW: A crude but accurate description, Trench.

TRENCH: So, is this the end?

EDITOR LAW: Oh no, not at all – don't worry about that. Max Sterling has given me his personal assurance that nothing will really change here at the Stokeham Herald.

SALLY-ANNE: If nothing's going to change, why's he bothering taking over then?

EDITOR LAW: Because, Sally-Anne, he's a businessman. Whatever else this Paper is, it makes money. Max respects and recognises that.

TRENCH: What about our jobs though?

EDITOR LAW: I told you, relax. Max has given his assurances that both your jobs are safe. Even I'm going to stay on as part-time editor but alas, I will have slightly more time for golf. The appropriate legally binding contracts will be drawn up ready for me to sign the Paper over tomorrow – at noon.

SALLY-ANNE: It's very kind of you, Editor Law, but you don't have to worry about me. I resign.

EDITOR LAW: Sorry?

TRENCH: Listen Sally, if it's because I made you see Darnia, then I'm sorry.

SALLY-ANNE: No, it's nothing to do with that; this take-over or even the delightful Dominic. I am leaving to live with Jonathan – in London.

TRENCH: *(Says almost dumbstruck:)* Oh.

SALLY-ANNE: Come on Trenchy, I was going to tell you when we were alone but suddenly, now seemed as good as time as ever.

TRENCH: When are you leaving?

SALLY-ANNE: Don't worry – not right now. I'll be around for a few more days yet.

EDITOR LAW: Well, thank-you for telling me, Sally-Anne. I'll inform Max that you, at least, will not be joining the new regime.

(Melancholy music moves a little bit of time on.)

(TRENCH and SALLY-ANNE are back in their office.)

TRENCH: I wonder where golden boy is?

SALLY-ANNE: Dominic? He's probably powdering his nose or something.

TRENCH: Yes, well we do know he never seems to leave the building.

SALLY-ANNE: If he did, he'd probably shrivel up and die in the fresh air. What a wonderful thought!

TRENCH: You know Dominic lied, don't you?

SALLY-ANNE: Do I?

TRENCH: Dominic previously claimed that Editor Law has told him of his intention to sell, when Law suggested he had told us two first.

SALLY-ANNE: He was probably lying to try and impress and sound superior. Adding two and two...

TRENCH: ... and making four on this occasion. Dominic was right, though. Mind you, he most likely gleaned his information from the rumour mill.

BLACK BOX: Take me to Gordon's DIY on the high street before fifteen hundred hours to discover your fifth clue.

SALLY-ANNE: Fifth clue? What about the fourth clue?

TRENCH: Well, either the Black Box has missed it out for a reason, or he can't count! Either way, we'd better be going – I don't want to be on the last second, for a change.

SALLY-ANNE: Trench, would you be offended if I don't come with you on this occasion? I'm feeling tired all of a sudden.

TRENCH: Are you all right?

SALLY-ANNE: Fine – probably still recovering from dodging Darnia's clutches! And, in any case, one of us had better get back to some mundane office work. Dominic's complaining enough as it is.

TRENCH: All right, I'll be off, *(he suddenly takes-off Darnia:)* darling.

(With a slight SALLY-ANNE giggle, TRENCH leaves the office and walks down the corridor.)

MAX: It's Trench, isn't it? Pleased to meet you at last.

TRENCH: Max Sterling, an unexpected... err encounter.

MAX: I'm just over here to chew a few things over with your editor ahead of tomorrow's 'seal the deal'.

TRENCH: And what plans do you have for the Stokeham Herald, Mr Sterling?

MAX: Max, please.

TRENCH: Max, then. This humble Paper has built a reputation for sometimes biting journalism in its forty odd year lifetime.

MAX: Oh, I have big plans for this Paper.

TRENCH: Really?

MAX: But don't look so concerned. They'll always be a position for you here, Trench.

(DOMINIC walks up to them in the corridor and stops.)

DOMINIC: It's an honour to meet you, sir.

(DOMINIC shakes MAX very warmly by the hand.)

MAX: Ditto Dominic. You may stop shaking my hand now.

DOMINIC: Oh, sorry.

MAX: Watch this bright young lad, Trench. His recent story on local car-parking problems was inspiring stuff. More, please.

DOMINIC: Thank-you, sir.

MAX: Don't you agree, Trench?

TRENCH: Oh yes, absolutely. In my journalistic experience, I find car parking up most people's street!

            (Quirky music changes the scene.)

            (We hear the door chime as TRENCH enters Gordon's DIY and walks to the counter.)

TRENCH: Gordon, it's me Trench – how are you doing?

GORDON: I'm fine – we're fine.

TRENCH: Where is Vicky?

GORDON: Studying hard at university. She'll be a legal eagle very soon. You're not checking up on me, are you Trench?

TRENCH: Oh no, no, no. I've come in here to buy something actually.

GORDON: That's good – most people do. Is it something I can help you with or do you just want to browse?

TRENCH: I'm looking for a black box.

GORDON: Are you sure you want a black box? You see, Trench, you seem to be carrying one under your arm.

TRENCH: Oh, not that one, Gordon. I'm looking for a very small black box – about so big.

BLACK BOX: The fifth clue: It is cocktail hour at the hardware store. You have ninety seconds remaining.

GORDON: It speaks!

TRENCH: *(Who whispers loudly to GORDON:)* Attention seeker – take no notice, you'll only encourage him.

GORDON: Back to tiny black boxes, I'm pretty sure we don't stock them – and I can't think who would…

TRENCH: Cocktail hour at the hardware store? What on earth does it mean by that?

GORDON: Vicky enjoys a cocktail occasionally, did you know?

TRENCH: Of course, that's it – a cocktail. What does your wife normally drink?

GORDON: Hmm, let me see.

TRENCH: Quick, quick.

GORDON: Sometimes a Blue Lagoon… sometimes a screwdriver…

BLACK BOX: You have twenty seconds remaining.

TRENCH: Screwdrivers, that's the things – where are they?

GORDON: Over there.

(TRENCH dashes to the screwdriver display.)

TRENCH: Excuse me madam, I have to get to that shelf.

SHOPPER: Well, really!

(TRENCH starts pulling the screwdrivers off the shelves, frantically searching.)

TRENCH: It must be on one of these shelves somewhere. Ah, there it is – the mini black box. Time to squeeze… A man… Some kind of model traffic warden, I think.

BLACK BOX: One second remaining.

(TRENCH drops the model and it disintegrates in a puff of smoke.)

GORDON: I say, what's been happening here?

             (Intriguing music ends the scene.)

OLD TOM: More tea, Trench? There's plenty left in the pot.

TRENCH: Don't mind if I do.

OLD TOM: I'll pour.

             (OLD TOM pours the tea.)

TRENCH: Can I ask you one thing, Old Tom? Why is there a tea cosy on the teapot?

OLD TOM: To keep the tea cold.

TRENCH: Ask a stupid question.

OLD TOM: Then I'll ask a sensible one: Who placed the clues in their diverse locations – and how?

TRENCH: Good question – and the clues themselves: Black sheep, sports car, crumpled-up paper and a traffic warden... Baffling, aren't they?

OLD TOM: But there must be a connection... And what happened to the mysteriously missing fourth clue?

TRENCH: And if that isn't enough – Sally-Anne has resigned to live with her boyfriend in London and Editor Law is signing over his newspaper to Max Sterling tomorrow at noon.

OLD TOM: It's all happening! And what about Dominic?

TRENCH: He's as irritating as ever.

OLD TOM: A Black Box; rushing around for bizarre, nonsensical clues – it's ridiculous, truly barmy.

TRENCH: Tell me about it, old timer.

OLD TOM: And locating all the clues, has still involved meeting people acquainted from our previous cases.

TRENCH: But why?

OLD TOM: I think that someone is playing a game with us. And if so, what is the purpose of the game? Who are the winners?

TRENCH: And who are the losers..?

              (A longer piece of mystery music indicates the end of Act Two.)

ACT THREE

(SALLY-ANNE and TRENCH are in their office.)

SALLY-ANNE: The calm before the storm.

TRENCH: You're not talking about Darnia again, are you?

SALLY-ANNE: Err no, Trench. I was referring to us being in the office before the dreaded Dominic arrives.

TRENCH: Then let's leave before he does make an appearance.

SALLY-ANNE: Where to, though? Your Black Box hasn't said a word yet. Or shall we just wander around aimlessly?

TRENCH: Old Tom said 'who placed the clues – and how?' So let's find out.

SALLY-ANNE: By visiting a previous clue-scene?

TRENCH: Yes, and let's visit the location that the clue-planter would have most likely been seen – sweet Sawn-Off's mother's house.

(Decisive music moves things on.)

(We hear TRENCH knock on the front door. The door opens after a few moments.)

MOTHER: Hello, it's Cedric's two young friends – I'm afraid he isn't in, though. He has returned to his lovely flower shop in London.

SALLY-ANNE: That's all right, Mrs err..?

MOTHER: Just call me Mother, my son does.

SALLY-ANNE: Mrs err... Mother, we just want a very quick chat with you.

MOTHER: Then you must come inside and this time I will make us all a nice cup of tea.

TRENCH: Err... we've just had morning tea... and then will have to investigate yet another story. But that's another story.

SALLY-ANNE: A local reporter's work is never done...

TRENCH: So, to save time – can I ask you one question?

MOTHER: Of course you can, young man – and I'll be as quick as I can because you are obviously two very busy bees!

TRENCH: Prior to our last visit, has anyone unusual visited you recently? A stranger, perhaps?

MOTHER: Hmm, no – I don't think so.

SALLY-ANNE: Any kind of visitor, then?

MOTHER: Let me think... Oh yes, the gas man came a day before you did.

TRENCH: Now, this is very important, did he go into your kitchen?

MOTHER: Yes, yes he did. In fact he insisted on making the tea, just like you did! I can make tea myself, you know – honestly.

SALLY-ANNE: And I'm sure it's lovely tea too, Mother.

MOTHER: Mother knows best.

TRENCH: And what did this gas-man look like?

MOTHER: He was tall like you, a fair bit younger though – and had a rather unruly mop of curly brown hair.

TRENCH: Thank-you, Mother – you've been most helpful.

MOTHER: Oh good.

SALLY-ANNE: Goodbye, Mother.

(MOTHER closes the front door after they leave.)

SALLY-ANNE: That description, Trench, sounds an awful lot like Dominic.

TRENCH: But why would Dominic want us to run around Stokeham carrying this Black Box to uncover bizarre, cryptic clues?

SALLY-ANNE: Some sort of twisted prank, that only he finds amusing?

TRENCH: He doesn't seem the type, though...

BLACK BOX: Take me to the telephone box on the High Street before eleven hundred and forty-five hours to discover your fourth and final clue.

SALLY-ANNE: The missing clue...

TRENCH: Let's go – and get it.

               (Traditional private-eye type music moves time on.)

SALLY-ANNE: There's the telephone kiosk.

TRENCH: And we're five minutes to spare. Oh no, there's
someone inside it.

SALLY-ANNE: She shouldn't be too long. We'll just have to wait.

               (Quick music emphasising impatience passes a few
more minutes.)

TRENCH: Stupid woman. There's no sign of her shutting-up,
typical.

SALLY-ANNE: Hey!

TRENCH: We've only a few minutes left.

SALLY-ANNE: I'll knock.

               (The kiosk door opens.)

TRENCH: Thank-you, madam. It's going to be a tight squeeze,
Sally-Anne – me, you... and the Black Box.

SALLY-ANNE: People might start talking. You go in, I'll 'keep guard'
outside.

TRENCH: At least I won't have to look very far for the clue.

               (TRENCH opens the door and goes inside.)

BLACK BOX: The fourth clue: A change is as good as a rest. You
have ninety seconds remaining.

               (The telephone rings. TRENCH opens the door slightly.)

TRENCH: Sally-Anne, the telephone's ringing – what shall I do?

SALLY-ANNE: Err, answer it?

TRENCH: Of course, thanks!

               (The door closes and TRENCH picks up the receiver.)

TRENCH: Hello, hello. Trench here, who is it?

GEOFFREY: *(Obviously speaking from the other end of the 'phone.)*
Trench, it's me – Geoffrey.

TRENCH: Who told you to 'phone here? Never mind, did you
recommend Dominic to us?

GEOFFREY: No way, do you know what happened at the
Ghoulmouth Gazette?

               *(Telephone interference can be heard. Foreboding
music changes the atmosphere. And we can no longer hear
GEOFFREY.)*

TRENCH: Speak up, Geoffrey – with all this interference I can
only just hear you. He didn't, he did. Never, sacked? Closed down? Oh
no, they'll do the same here.

BLACK BOX: Twenty seconds remaining.

TRENCH: I'll have to go, Geoffrey. I'll be in touch. Yes, I got that:
'message received, accepted and understood' – just.

               (TRENCH puts the 'phone down.)

TRENCH: Now, what was the clue? A change is as good...
Change, of course, look at the returned coins collector... and there is
the little black box.

               (We hear TRENCH squeeze the mini black box open.)

TRENCH: A red and white striped pole.

BLACK BOX: One second remaining.

> (*TRENCH drops the pole before it explodes and dashes out of the telephone box.*)

SALLY-ANNE: What was all that about?

TRENCH: We have less than fifteen minutes to save the Stokeham Herald. Come on, Sally-Anne – we're going to have to really dash. It's nearly noon.

SALLY-ANNE: You do the dashing, Trench – I'll catch you up at the Herald. You'll be faster without me. (*She turns round.*) Oops, he's already gone.

> (*Fast paced music which also heightens suspense ends the scene.*)

> (*TRENCH is furiously running down the corridors of the Stokeham Herald.*)

TRENCH: Come on, Trench. Barely seconds left...

> (*TRENCH bursts through EDITOR LAW's office door.*)

TRENCH: (*Who's breathless but loud.*) Editor Law, do not sign that document.

EDITOR LAW: What's going on?

DOMINIC: Ah, good old Trench – you're just in time... to be too late. The ink may not be dry yet, but Editor Law has signed. The Paper is ours.

TRENCH: Ours?

MAX: Yes, I, Max Sterling and my business partner Dominic Jenkins, now own the Stokeham Herald.

EDITOR LAW: I don't understand.

MAX: It's really quite simple, Editor Law – or should I say ex-Editor Law. Hand the letters out, Dominic.

DOMINIC: Yes, sir.

EDITOR LAW: What are they?

MAX: Your redundancy notices.

EDITOR LAW: But you promised that our jobs were safe.

MAX: I lied. Look at it this way, now you have more time than ever to play your infernal golf.

TRENCH: Question: how can we be redundant, when our jobs still exist?

MAX: They won't. We have taken over this Paper for one purpose only: to demolish it; and build a multi-storey car park in its place. This is the business myself and Dominic are in. We go around the country and have 'transformed' many places – it's highly profitable. Local newspaper businesses usually make ideal establishments because they are normally located at prime sites close to the town centre.

TRENCH: So, that's why you were banging on about car parking problems so much.

MAX: That's right, create a demand...

TRENCH: But why pick on this particular newspaper?

DOMINIC: Your friend, Geoffrey in all innocence recommended you to us – before we sacked him and went on to close down the Ghoulmouth Gazette, of course. You're still holding my Black Box, Trench – how quaint.

TRENCH: Your Black Box, Dominic? Care to explain?

DOMINIC: A diversion, Trench. An extravagant, theatrical, ridiculous and ultimately an amusing one – but simply a diversion nonetheless. Geoffrey also let slip about you and Old Tom solving mysteries and the like, so I knew I had to keep you more than occupied whilst myself and sir got on with serious business of car-parking your newspaper. I made the Black Box. It contains a microprocessor, sound recorder, speaker and voice relay – see when I speak into my little microphone: *(DOMINIC speaks, but his voice comes through electronically via the BLACK BOX:)* I am the Black Box – and you, Trench are a fool.

TRENCH: I've certainly been fooled.

DOMINIC: Believe it or not myself and Max are sportsmen, so we, in the interests of fair play, decided to give you a chance. You could have worked our intentions out from the tantalising clues left, if you discovered them on time. Even the last clue was timed so you could have just prevented the take-over, if you had been fast enough. But, of course Trench, you were too slow, far too slow.

TRENCH: What do you want me to say, Dominic – how clever you are?

DOMINIC: It would be nice. I also found it amusing, after studying past copies of the Stokeham Herald, to involve people from your previous investigations.

TRENCH: You shouldn't have gone to so much trouble, but you do know about Old Tom. How much do you know?

DOMINIC: Know about Old Tom? I even visited him.

TRENCH: You couldn't have – you don't know where he lives.

DOMINIC: The Black Box also contains a satellite navigation locator – so the box led me back to Mayflower Court. And that's when I really felt sorry for you, Trench.

TRENCH: Felt sorry for me?

DOMINIC: Old Tom doesn't even exist. His supposed Flat was derelict – and empty.

TRENCH: I don't believe you.

SALLY-ANNE: I'm here! Have I missed all the fun?

TRENCH: We have lost the Stokeham Herald, Sally.

MAX: And you are all sacked. So, if you don't mind..?

DOMINIC: Trench, leave my Black Box on your way out.

TRENCH: Might as well, no use to me now. Err, no – you know what they say about 'finder's keepers'?

DOMINIC: Suit yourself. Right, all of you out. Get out!

      (Sad music suggesting loss and defeat closes the scene.)

      (We hear TRENCH rattle the front door.)

TRENCH: It's no use – the doors locked. I know – letter box. *(We hear him open the letter box.)* The hall's not only empty but stripped bare. Old Tom must have left, assuming he does actually exist... Am I going mad?

OLD TOM: Come in, young man, the door is open.

      (TRENCH tries the door again, this time it opens. He puts something down in the hallway and enters the living room.)

TRENCH: Why's the hallway completely empty?

OLD TOM: I'll tell you later, now sit down, Trench. Traffic warden, crumpled paper, sports car and a black sheep. Someone's been sending us on a right old wild goose chase.

TRENCH: Old Tom, I've something to tell you.

OLD TOM: The fourth clue? Go ahead then.

TRENCH: Oh that? I'd almost forgotten. It was a thin, red and white pole about so big.

OLD TOM: A pole... or a barrier? I think I've got it, Trench. The black sheep of the family; a snake in the grass; a traitor from within, if you like. An enemy who has deliberately plotted against us...

TRENCH: That'll be Dominic.

OLD TOM: What do sports cars do?

TRENCH: Take over?

OLD TOM: Exactly. The crumpled-up newspaper illustrates the folding of the Stokeham Herald. The traffic warden could quite easily be a car-park attendant and the pole an entrance/exit barrier to surprisingly... a car park. The Stokeham Herald must be in grave danger, Trench – you had better rush before, before... But judging from your expression and the fact that it is now well after mid-day – we're too late, aren't we?

TRENCH: I'm afraid so, but at least we know now why the fourth clue was held over – it meant contact with Geoffrey who would have warned me about the car-parking leeches Max Sterling and Dominic Jenkins – they killed the Ghoulmouth Gazette prior to picking on us.

OLD TOM: But why did they pick on you?

TRENCH: I've already kind of told you. Geoffrey inadvertently mentioned us and the Paper.

OLD TOM: It still doesn't make sense. Ghoulmouth is the other side of the country. True, they might have reached Stokeham eventually, but why come straight here? Of course, that's the reason.

TRENCH: Not for the first time, you've lost me, Old Tom.

OLD TOM: Think about our very first case. Think about who we really upset by saving the Mayflower flats. Think about Dominic. Come on- think, Trench, think.

TRENCH: Yes, yes – now I know why – but I still can't see it helping. My job, the Herald has gone – lost forever. This is one case where we are well and truly beaten, Old Tom. And it pains me to say – outwitted.

OLD TOM: I agree, we have badly lost a battle, but the war isn't over just yet... I assume Dominic asked for the Black Box back, but you didn't give it him.

TRENCH: I nearly did, but decided to keep it just to annoy him – hang on, how did you..? I know, like before you heard me place something in the hall and deduced it was our boxed friend.

OLD TOM: Fetch it then – along with that hammer you most kindly bought me – as you know it resides in the kitchen drawer. I knew it would come in useful one day.

TRENCH: What are you going to do?

OLD TOM: This time, my observational deductive process hasn't quite worked out. So, we are going to give brute force a damned good try for a change...

        (Determined music changes the scene.)

        (The office door opens, MAX and DOMINIC are discussing something whilst looking at the plans. Rustling of paper can be heard.)

MAX: Yes Dominic, I thought the main car-parking terminals are going to be here – and here. Trench, Sally-Anne and good old ex-Editor Law, quite a visiting committee. None of you, however, have any right to be here – so please leave, as you can see we are very busy.

TRENCH: Sorry to interrupt you Max, I've come to return what's left of the Back Box to Dominic.

          (A rattling sound can be heard as TRENCH hands the bag of BLACK BOX broken bits to DOMINIC.)

DOMINIC: I shall sue you for criminal damage, Trench.

SALLY-ANNE: That was very naughty of you, Trenchy.

EDITOR LAW: Unforgiveable...

DOMINIC: Oh, shut up and get out. All of you.

TRENCH: I know now why you chose this newspaper. You were probably quite happily illegally and dishonestly slowly closing down local papers to replace them with very useful car-parks pretty much at random. But Geoffrey no doubt triggered a memory, a memory perhaps of ex-Sergeant Jenkins?

DOMINIC: All right, I admit it – it can do you no good. Ex-Sergeant Jenkins, as you put it, and for some reason passionately wanted Mayflower Court to be demolished. But of course, your goody goody Stokeham Herald campaign stopped that. He died shortly afterwards - sad and alone. I blame you for his death. You broke his spirit – my uncle.

TRENCH: So, that's why you said 'the Black Box brought you back to Mayflower Court'. You had previously visited your uncle there.

DOMINIC: Bravo, Trench. And revenge is sweet, conning Editor Law to sell this Paper as a going concern, only to tarmac it, was may I say, a very, very pleasurable days' work.

TRENCH: Oh, sorry Dominic and Mr Max, I forgot to mention that I did save one thing from the Black Box – the sound recorder. From the box of delights, something delightful...

(TRENCH presses 'play' and DOMINIC's recorded voice can be heard.)

DOMINIC: (From the tape-recorder:) ...conning Editor Law to sell this Paper, as a going concern, only to tarmac...

(TRENCH presses 'stop'.)

TRENCH: Did you hear that, Sergeant Strong?

(SERGEANT STRONG enters the office.)

SERGEANT STRONG: Yes, I did and together with the other evidence we have collected from around the country means that I can declare this newspaper sale legally void. Max Sterling and Dominic Jenkins, you are under arrest for numerous accounts of obtaining property by deception and for other offences – when I've thought of them.

MAX: I warned you, Dominic that it would be too dangerous here. And as for you and that fancy box of tricks... I knew it wouldn't work.

DOMINIC: Max, do us all a favour, will you? And shut up.

SALLY-ANNE: Wait, before they go, I think Editor Law wants to do something right in front of their eyes.

EDITOR LAW: Do I, Sally? Yes, of course I do. This is – or was the contract selling the Stokeham Herald to your bad selves.

(We can hear EDITOR LAW gleefully tearing the contract to pieces, with TRENCH and SALLY-ANNE cheering on.)

(Lighter music ends the scene.)

SALLY-ANNE: I've said goodbye to Editor Law, now it's your turn, Trench.

TRENCH: First, Sally-Anne, there is something I must do.

(We hear TRENCH grab SALLY-ANNE and give her a long kiss.)

TRENCH: Maybe I should have done that when we first met. Maybe things would have turned out differently...

SALLY-ANNE: You know, if you would have knocked on my door at Fisherman's Cove, you would have found it open... But you were too wrapped up in Old Tom's latest mystery.

TRENCH: That just about sums us up.

SALLY-ANNE: With Old Tom around in spirit, at least, meant that me and you never had a chance.

TRENCH: But now you are going to have a new life with Jonathan in London. What are you actually going to do there?

SALLY-ANNE: I was going to ask around for a job as a television news reporter, maybe at Globelink News, but a little addition to our lives has forced us to change plans.

TRENCH: An addition to you and Jonathan? Are you going to have a threesome? (He then takes off DARNIA:) I adore threesomes!

SALLY-ANNE: (Who laughs:) Yes, 'Darnia'. It is a threesome in a way, I suppose. Me and Jonathan are going to have a baby.

TRENCH: That's great, truly great.

SALLY-ANNE: Goodbye, Trench.

(Music tinged with sadness closes the scene.)

OLD TOM: Come in, young man, the door is open.

(TRENCH enters the flat.)

TRENCH: Now there's nothing left in the whole flat apart from your armchair – and my chair. What is going on, Old Tom?

OLD TOM: First, Trench, sit down and tell me what happened.

TRENCH: (Who sits down.) Your plan worked a treat, old timer. Max and Dominic are arrested and the Stokeham Herald is saved. Sally-Anne has left for pastures new and nest building in London. And Editor Law has found a way to play more golf without selling the Paper: he's promoted me to be Assistant Editor.

OLD TOM: Congratulations. I suppose you will need to employ some new reporters?

TRENCH: Yes, interviews start very soon for one vacancy. The other, I've offered to Geoffrey. Well, he's obviously lost his job at the Gazette and his insurance work has dried up.

OLD TOM: So, he said yes?

TRENCH: Well, Geoffers actually said, 'message...' – never mind, he starts next week. He'll probably drive me mad, but after Dominic I'll take the chance. And now, are you going to tell me about the mystery of your vanishing furniture?

OLD TOM: First, look under your chair.

TRENCH: Two cups of cold tea. Here's yours. (They start drinking.)

OLD TOM: I'm moving on, Trench. You've been promoted, your partner's left. It is the end of an era. You don't need me anymore. I can be of no further use to you. You have come a long way, my boy, learnt a great deal. You will not look at things quite the same from hence forth. My work here is complete. You will not see me again.

TRENCH: But who are you, Old Tom? You have never said.

OLD TOM: I think that some mysteries are best left unsolved. Don't you think that knowing would somehow spoil the magic?

TRENCH: Yes, yes I suppose it would. So, the armchair detective has solved his last ever case, then?

OLD TOM: You have finished your tea, Trench – it is time.

TRENCH: Yes, I'm sorry – I'd better go.

OLD TOM: We've had some fun, though.

          ('The Armchair Detective' mystery music starts playing in the background.)

OLD TOM: We discovered that it was Jill Masterson manipulating events behind Mayflower Court...

TRENCH: ... and that Marcus Dreadbury's missing fiancé was a lot closer to his manor-house home than we first suspected...

OLD TOM: ... and the best celebrity stalkers always turn out to be the spouse...

TRENCH   ... the brothers Quinn mystery at Fisherman's Cove was a family affair...

OLD TOM: ... and we unlocked Gordon's psychological secret...

TRENCH: - and shopped a shoplifter! And, finally, found that it was Max and Dominic who were behind a dastardly revenge plot to pave paradise – err the Stokeham Herald – and put up a parking lot. Funny, that sounds like a song.

(The background music fades away.)

(We hear the remarkable sound of OLD TOM rising…)

TRENCH: Old Tom, you've stood up – from your armchair! What's happening?

OLD TOM: I cannot abide people lolling around on chairs all day! Come on, stand up man – I'm here to shake your hand.

TRENCH: I'm speechless, but I will rise to the occasion.

(TRENCH gets up, and they warmly shake hands.)

TRENCH: Old Tom, I would like to thank…

OLD TOM: No, Trench – there's really no need. There is only one more thing we need to say to each other – and we don't require a clue from any black box to know what that is, do we?

TRENCH: No, no we don't. Here goes then…

TRENCH & OLD TOM: Farewell, old friend.

CLOSING MYSTERY MUSIC

DOMINIC JENKINS

MAX STERLING

BLACK BOX

JILL MASTERSON

SAWN-OFF

DARNIA STORM

GORDON

GEOFFREY

MOTHER

SHOPPER

SERGEANT STRONG

'Boxed Set' Extras

The Man Behind The Armchair

Interview with author, Ian Shimwell

Interviewer: Tell us about your writing history.

Author: OK, I naturally loved English and Literature at school and pursued that in further education etc. Over the years, I have written many different things from short stories to novellas and covered genres such as science fiction, historical adventure, horror and mysteries. Eventually, I began to write three-act scripts based on favourite series such as _The Avengers_ and _Blakes' 7_.

So, what made you move from Steed and Blake to Old Tom?

Well, after what I humbly considered to be successful scripts of those shows, I wanted to write one that was completely mine. Having eventually done that, I decided I was happy with it and felt it had the potential to be developed into a series.

Going back to the pilot script, what was your inspiration for writing The Armchair Detective?

Unusually for me (I normally read grown-up fiction, honestly!), I was reading several children's novels from the series *The Invisible Detective* by Justin Richards. (These are excellent mystery adventure novels and I recommend them to anyone.) The element that inspired me was that the small group of children had created a shadowy, make-believe detective – who 'sat' in an armchair, whom the children used as a front to solve the mysteries.

Also, on television at the time, I was enjoying detective shows such as *Dangerous Davies - The Last Detective* and *New Tricks*. I sometimes found them more interesting when the mysteries dared to be of a more trivial nature.

Lastly, I fell in love with Lois from *Lois and Clark - The New Adventures of Superman*. I especially enjoyed their investigative drive and also the witty, biting banter between the pair.

So, I decided to write a pilot script that incorporated some of those elements – and more.

I wanted the stories to be small-scale but have the ambition to tell absorbing mysteries that could range from say complications from searching for a missing person to something as personal as someone not being themselves. I also tried to write it with a light touch – be witty, biting, funny and dramatic in turn whilst being true to the central core of the mystery.

Dare I ask who Old Tom is? And why is Trench the only one with contact?

Old Tom is my armchair detective who never rises from his armchair. I decided to write the scripts with the audio medium in mind, so I felt that having him a) chair-bound and b) contactable only by Trench, my main character - would be a great narrative device. Also Trench's chats with Old Tom could frame each of the three acts and drive the narrative forward in a thought-provoking way.

Once I had developed all the regular characters and the format, certain questions would surface concerning the underlying mythology of the series: Who is Old Tom? Why is he seen by no one other than Trench? Does he really exist? What of Old Tom's past – what has made him like this? What did he put his brilliant mind to back in his prime? Maybe some answers to these questions would be hinted at as the series progressed…

The Armchair Detective's Last Ever Case *was certainly an enthralling end to the series.*

Thanks!

Why was the capable, and my personal favourite, Sally-Anne written out?

Along with the idea of this final play weaving aspects of the previous five stories together, I wanted something else to give the series a sense of closure. I was also sorry to see Sally-Anne go, but her departure gave even more drama and unpredictability to the final script – and was another reason for Trench to move on without Old Tom.

So, is this really the end for Trench and Old Tom?

Check the website! (Or see my answers below.)

Are you working on any other projects?

Yes, I am in the process of developing and writing more *Armchair Detectives* as well adding to *The Novella Range* and *Classic Scripts.*

Can you give any more detail?

A major new character will be introduced for *The Armchair Detective* that will have far-reaching consequences for Trench and Old Tom. *The Novella Range* will soon experience the wonder of science fiction and a brooding murder mystery. And the greatest detective of them all may soon visit *Classic Scripts.*

Any plans for an actual novel?

Not as yet, but it is something I hope to achieve at some stage.

Thank-you!

Deleted Scenes

Deleted Scene One:

This scene would have taken place from **The Armchair Detective On Holiday** *Act Three (page 182) after the scene ending with:* TRENCH: And that's what I find very curious… (*Curious music ends this scene.*) - *and would have been as follows:*

> (*We can just make out some conference speeches in the background.*)

SALLY-ANNE: You're so lucky Editor Law has just seen you. Somehow, he thinks you've been here all morning!

TRENCH: I know. Our boss may have his faults, but as far as pulling the wool – please, we must keep him forever, at all costs!

SALLY-ANNE: Err, can you see what I can see, Trench?

TRENCH: Only the receptionist fellow looking rather blank.

SALLY-ANNE: But can you see beyond that?

TRENCH: Sally-Anne, wouldn't this be a bit easier if you told me what you are getting at? You know, in plain English.

SALLY-ANNE: All right. Peeping through the doorway into the back room, I can just make out several books.

TRENCH: What's up, desperate for a holiday read?

SALLY-ANNE: Not quite. They look to me like the hotel books – very useful information could be gleaned from them. And they are bounded.

TRENCH: Bounded eh, at least let's hope they are binding… Sall, you create a diversion by acting daft or something and I'll slip behind the counter and take a peek.

SALLY-ANNE: Why does it always have to be me?

TRENCH: Err, you're good at acting daft..?

(A stony silence greets TRENCH.)

TRENCH: Tell you what, I'll keep him occupied while you sneak in there, then.

SALLY-ANNE: That's better.

(TRENCH walks up to the receptionist.)

TRENCH: Excuse me, I'm supposed to be meeting a couple of friends here. Could you check if they've arrived. *(The receptionist nods.)* Thanks – they go by the name of the brothers Quinn…

SALLY-ANNE: *(Who whispers:)* I'm in.

(Music illustrating the dangers of getting caught, changes the scene.)

The story would have then continued with: (We hear the usual background noises associated with a hotel restaurant.) SALLY-ANNE: The Sandy Star does make a lovely lunch. I'll give them that.

Also, Sally-Anne explaining that (during lunch with Trench and Geoffrey) she slipped into the hotel office while the hotel manager was listening to the keynote speech would have been replaced with a brief summary of the above.

I, reluctantly, dropped this scene for timing reasons as I wanted the pace of Act Three to start picking up and edging ever quicker to the final revelation. Shame though, there were funny bits; it showcased Sally-Anne's observational drive and it moved forward the narrative. At least now, you can enjoy it in all its glory.

Deleted Scene Two:

*In **The Armchair Detective and the Psychological Secret**
Act Three (page 231), this short scene replaces the section after:*
TRENCH: What? How?

MRS HOPKINS: He left a roller-skate in the middle of
the hall.

TRENCH: Really? How shocking.

MRS HOPKINS: *(Ignoring TRENCH.)* Father came home
from work and stepped on it.

SALLY-ANNE: Am I right in pre-supposing he wasn't
wearing his crash helmet?

MRS HOPKINS: Father has a terrible fall. We had only
just bought a small but solid oak table for the telephone…
A quite exquisite antique, actually.

TRENCH: I think you'll have to elaborate slightly
further, Mrs Hopkins.

MRS HOPKINS: My husband cracked his skull on the
oak table. Blood running down the grain…

TRENCH: A freak but fatal accident.

The story would have then continued with: SALLY-ANNE: How awful. You did convince Gordon, though, that it wasn't his fault, just a terrible accident?

I changed this section because the added comedic elements perhaps detracted from the tragic events and the chat with Mrs Hopkins was becoming over long. Also, having Father trip over Gordon (at the top of the stairs) gave the cause of his death a more personal involvement from Gordon and an added motive for Mrs Hopkins to dislike her son.

Easter Egg

Rearrange the following anagram to reveal the author's first rule for writing The Armchair Detective:

Sen. nice nervy heretics.

In true 'hangman' style, the answer is as follows: (6,2,2,5,5)

------/--/--/-----/-----

Check out *The Armchair Detective* Secret Webpage for the answer.

(With thanks to HS.)

Secret Webpage

For an exciting *Armchair Detective* news exclusive, follow this link:

http://thearmchairdetective.moonfruit.com

and click on the small 'Secret Webpage' link at the bottom left hand corner of the Home page.

This information is only accessible by following the above – so it really is secret!

Favourite Quotes

OLD TOM: Come in, young man, the door is open.
Most Armchair Detectives

SALLY-ANNE: What are you, an old folk's home revolutionary or something? *The Armchair Detective*

TRENCH: I assume you've not kidnapped to ask me directions, so what's this all about? *The Armchair Detective*

TRENCH: …it was just before I set foot in this pub where I overheard a rather interesting conversation.

SALLY-ANNE: Like when the price of crisps are going up next? *The Armchair Detective and the Manor-House Mystery*

OLD TOM: Lightening never strikes twice, young Trench but then again, history does have an unpleasant habit of repeating itself. *The Armchair Detective and the Manor-House Mystery*

TRENCH: That Sawn-Off saw off Emmy? *The Armchair Detective and the Manor-House Mystery*

TRENCH: Well, if you think seventeen rooms in your abode is humble, I'd hate to see you when you're being arrogant. *The Armchair Detective and the Manor-House Mystery*

OLD TOM: There is nothing more mysterious than a locked room in a manor-house… *The Armchair Detective and the Manor-House Mystery*

TRENCH: Not so much as a skeleton in the cupboard – this one resides in the whole bedroom! *The Armchair Detective and the Manor-House Mystery*

HAPPY: Me happy. *The Armchair Detective and the Manor-House Mystery*

OLD TOM: Deductions enlighten many a shadowy corner. *The Armchair Detective and the Manor-House Mystery*

EDITOR LAW: …may I introduce you to, Miss Darnia Storm.

(We hear sharp intakes of breath as the sound of DARNIA's stilettoes are heard entering the office.)

SALLY-ANNE: Close your mouth, Trench. Electric fly-traps are all that's necessary for this building. *The Armchair Detective and the Celebrity Stalker*

DARNIA: Right, that's enough about me – even though myself is my favourite subject. *The Armchair Detective and the Celebrity Stalker*

SALLY-ANNE: This is a very sleepy village, Trench – perhaps they were all asleep! *The Armchair Detective On Holiday*

SALLY-ANNE: Well, you'll just have to talk to me instead. You can pretend I'm Old Tom, if you like! *The Armchair Detective On Holiday*

TRENCH: I don't think we are actually going to find them. Hide-and-seek games don't usually last fifty years! *The Armchair Detective On Holiday*

TRENCH: Wait, I think there's a commotion in men's clothing. *The Armchair Detective and the Psychological Secret*

SALLY-ANNE: Daddy Hopkins went head over heels… into oblivion. *The Armchair Detective and the Psychological Secret*

OLD TOM: Nothing lasts forever, Trench. When the time is right, I will move on – and so will you… *The Armchair Detective and the Psychological Secret*

TRENCH: And don't call my Black Box ridiculous, you'll hurt his feelings! *The Armchair Detective's Last Ever Case*

TRENCH: So, is this the end? *The Armchair Detective's Last Ever Case*

TRENCH: In my journalistic experience, I find car parking up most people's street! *The Armchair Detective's Last Ever Case*

SALLY-ANNE: With Old Tom around in spirit, at
least, meant that me and you (Trench) never had a chance.
The Armchair Detective's Last Ever Case

OLD TOM: I think that some mysteries are best left
unsolved. *The Armchair Detective's Last Ever Case*

OLD TOM: I cannot abide people lolling around
on chairs all day! *The Armchair Detective's Last Ever Case*

OLD TOM: Come on. Think Trench, think. *Most
Armchair Detectives*

Message from Old Tom

Finally, we come to the end. I am suitably humbled that you have followed all my investigations with Trench. I hope you have enjoyed them half as much as I did solving them (with a little help from my friend).

Please take the trouble to visit the official *Armchair Detective* website, not only you will discover more about me, but I post my own monthly mystery on there, and I challenge you to crack them. So, it's worth regularly checking back.

Dear reader, I now only have two further things to mention:

Farewell, old friends.

And…

You can get up from *your* armchair now!

Old Tom

www.thearmchairdetective.moonfruit.com

Ingram Content Group UK Ltd.
Milton Keynes UK
UKHW041832240323
419150UK00012B/304/J